THE EARTH
IS MY
MOTHER

BEV DOOLITTLE

THE EARTH
IS MY
MOTHER

AND ELISE MACLAY

THE GREENWICH WORKSHOP PRESS

To Dorothy, my mother. —B.D.
To Elise, my mother. —E.M.

•

ISBN 0-86713-044-X
Library of Congress Cataloging-in-Publication
Data is available from the publisher

•

Other books by Bev Doolittle with Elise Maclay: *The Art of Bev Doolittle* and *New Magic*.
Visit our website to learn more about Doolittle's limited edition fine art prints, and to find the
location of the authorized Greenwich Workshop dealer nearest you:
www.greenwichworkshop.com

•

Greenwich Workshop Press books are distributed to
the trade by Artisan, a division of Workman Publishing.

•

Design by Peter Landa and Milly Iacono
Printed in China by Toppan
First Printing 2000

03 02 01 00   5 4 3 2

THE EARTH
IS MY
MOTHER

In early spring, when there is still snow on the highest peaks,
Magic Canyon seems most like its name, a magic place filled
with the sound of water, falling from great heights, bubbling merrily over smooth stones, collecting in deep,
quiet pools. Hidden trails and passageways lead in
and out of the canyon, but they are hard to find.
The Indians knew them all. So did Sarah.
She looked at her watch. Late.
She should have started for
home half an hour ago.
But whenever she
went out with
her camera,

time seemed to evaporate, especially in Magic Canyon. Luckily she knew a short cut, a secret passage between two huge boulders. She put the lens cap on her camera, put it away, and squeezed through the ancient crack, a shortcut her mother said was millions of years old.

Sarah Star Stewart was eleven and as long as she could remember she had loved Magic Canyon. As a tiny baby she went there almost daily, peeping out from under the sunshade of the special backpack her mother had designed for carrying her. The backpack was pale blue canvas and on it Sarah's mother had embroidered Indian symbols for sun, moon, beauty and courage. Sarah's father had been amused and puzzled. Sun, moon and beauty, he could understand. But courage? For a girl?

Especially for a girl, Sarah's mother said.

The backpack had outside pockets for camera and film and straps to hold Sarah securely upright when her mother left the trail and climbed up or down a steep slope to get the perfect photograph.

Sarah's mother was Abigail Stewart, the photographer, and she never tired of photographing Magic Canyon.

"It's my Giverny," she said. When Sarah was old enough to understand, her mother had told her about the French painter, Claude Monet, and the corner of

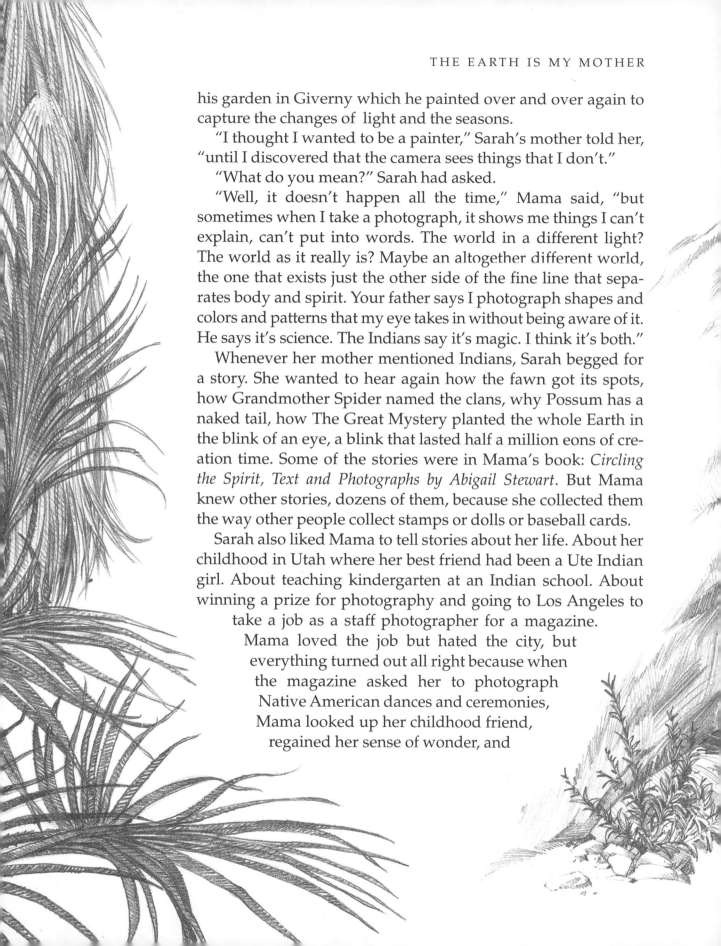

his garden in Giverny which he painted over and over again to capture the changes of light and the seasons.

"I thought I wanted to be a painter," Sarah's mother told her, "until I discovered that the camera sees things that I don't."

"What do you mean?" Sarah had asked.

"Well, it doesn't happen all the time," Mama said, "but sometimes when I take a photograph, it shows me things I can't explain, can't put into words. The world in a different light? The world as it really is? Maybe an altogether different world, the one that exists just the other side of the fine line that separates body and spirit. Your father says I photograph shapes and colors and patterns that my eye takes in without being aware of it. He says it's science. The Indians say it's magic. I think it's both."

Whenever her mother mentioned Indians, Sarah begged for a story. She wanted to hear again how the fawn got its spots, how Grandmother Spider named the clans, why Possum has a naked tail, how The Great Mystery planted the whole Earth in the blink of an eye, a blink that lasted half a million eons of creation time. Some of the stories were in Mama's book: *Circling the Spirit, Text and Photographs by Abigail Stewart*. But Mama knew other stories, dozens of them, because she collected them the way other people collect stamps or dolls or baseball cards.

Sarah also liked Mama to tell stories about her life. About her childhood in Utah where her best friend had been a Ute Indian girl. About teaching kindergarten at an Indian school. About winning a prize for photography and going to Los Angeles to take a job as a staff photographer for a magazine. Mama loved the job but hated the city, but everything turned out all right because when the magazine asked her to photograph Native American dances and ceremonies, Mama looked up her childhood friend, regained her sense of wonder, and

began what turned out to be a lifetime of study.

An article in *Image Magazine* said, "Abigail Stewart uses her camera to shine a light on ancient and joyful ways to live in harmony with the earth."

When Sarah was born, Mama continued her work, but instead of traveling all over the Southwest, she began photographing Magic Canyon in greater and greater depth. "It's fun to travel," she said, "but this canyon is older than time and filled with marvels."

Sarah and her mother talked often about Magic Canyon, what it hid and what it revealed. They talked about the Indians who lived there long ago, about the petroglyphs on its rock walls, about songs and ceremonies that drifted and echoed in the air, about ancient truths that never stop being true no matter what's on tele-vision or the Internet.

Magic Canyon was the best place to tell stories because in the canyon, words turned into birds and animals, flowers and wind and gold leaves fluttered from the cottonwood trees sing-ing and dancing, and before they knew it Sarah and Mama were singing and dancing, too. Sometimes

Sarah started it. Usually Mama did, jumping up, clapping her hands and singing their private willy-nilly silly secret song:

Hum and whistle, shout ho hi,
Crouch down low, jump to the sky,
Prance with your feet, let your arms fly,
Slither like a snake, buzz like a bee,
Everything dances, so do we.

Sometimes instead of prancing and flying and slithering and buzzing, they would howl or pounce or hop and make each other guess, what am I? Coyote. Mountain lion. Jackrabbit.

Once Sarah stood absolutely still with her arms outstretched. "What am I?"

Mama thought hard and finally said she hadn't a clue.

"I'm a hummingbird," Sarah said.

"But," Mama said, "hummingbirds flutter their wings—so fast it looks as if they're not moving at all."

"I know," Sarah said, laughing.

Mama laughed, too, so hard she had to sit down on a rocky ledge. Sarah flopped down beside her and for a long time they rested in silence. Then Mama spoke a thought she was having and it turned into a story, as often happened in Magic Canyon.

This time it was a true story about a woman named Hummingbird. "I photographed and interviewed her for a book that I began but never finished. I might go back to it someday. I was going to call it *Messengers of the Moon.*"

The name enchanted Sarah who wanted to know what it meant. Mama said the book was to be about Native American women who were spiritual leaders. They saw themselves as carriers of life and guardians of truths as ancient as Grandmother Moon. Hummingbird, Mama said, was a great Cahuilla healer, very old when Mama met her, but strong and full of life, busy from sunup to sunset gathering herbs and performing healing ceremonies and teaching earth secrets to her daughter who was called Hummingbird Speaking.

To be in the canyon with Mama was to be in a world where time dissolved and blended into a multicolored sea of delight. The past and the future were as available as the present, and life was a shimmering circle of light.

Sarah's father liked the canyon, too, but in a different way. He hiked for exercise, for fresh air, to conquer heights and thorns and rock slides, to feel a good kind of tiredness when he got home.

He might be at the house now, waiting for her, worrying.

It seemed to Sarah that before her mother died, her father had never worried. Now he worried a lot. She wished he wouldn't because she didn't go "hiking in the desert alone," as he put it. She just went to Magic Canyon, the most familiar place in the world. And she wasn't really alone. There were the animals. And there was Mama.

The canyon was full of memories so sharp and clear she didn't even have to close her eyes to imagine that they were together, she and Mama, doing the things they used to do. Now with the mouth of the canyon behind her and the trail widening out and losing itself on the flat desert floor, she felt Mama beside her. This was the running place.

"Race you to the house," Mama used to say and they would be off, galloping, galloping hoo, ha, hey! Even with her camera bag lumping out of her pack, Mama looked like a beautiful wild mare. Sarah, lifting her feet and stretching out her legs, pretended to be a frisky colt.

Because they weren't really racing they usually reached the house at the same time. As soon as they did, their flowing manes became hair again and their hooves became feet. They sat side by side on an old pine bench beside the door to take their boots off so they wouldn't track sand inside. If you did, the sand went *screech, screech* on the tile and scratched it.

Once Sarah told her mother that she wished the animals would come down from the canyon to visit. "I'd open the door for them," she said, "but I don't think they would come in."

"Probably not," Mama said. "The house is too full of things that animals have no use for. Refrigerator, clothes washer, electric iron, television. It must seem like a wasteland to them. Nothing juicy, sweet-smelling or blowing about in the wind."

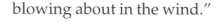

"When I grow up," Sarah said, "I'm going to build a house that the animals will love. It will be way out in the desert, made of huge boulders so from a distance you don't know it's there. Some of the rooms will be cool, shady caves, others will be sunny terraces, and there'll be two pools, one to swim in and a shallow one for the animals to drink from. The garage will be at the bottom of the mountain, underground, and people will have to walk or take a golf cart to get to the front door." Even as she listened to herself describing the house, Sarah seemed to hear other voices, her teacher's, her father's, saying, not unkindly but tinged with gentle disapproval, "Now you're getting silly, Sarah."

But Mama was following every word, her eyes shining. "What a good idea," she said. "You'll do it, too, I bet."

Mama had made the house sound possible. She made everything sound possible—and fun. That was why Sarah could not bear to let her memory fade or slip away as it sometimes did at home, in the bus, at school, in the supermarket or in front of the TV. That was why she had to go to Magic Canyon. It was the one place Sarah knew she would always be able to find her mother's spirit, singing and dancing in the air, making Sarah want to sing and dance, too, because in the canyon it was easy to believe the most important thing Mama had ever told her— that life is a circle and circles have no end. So if you love some-

one, they are part of you forever because you, the person you love, and all the animals and birds and fish and flowers and rocks and trees are connected, flowing into each other in the great glittering sun-rising never-ending circle of life.

Mama had been dead for almost a year now and Sarah's father said it was important for them to honor her memory by living bravely and joyfully as she would want them to. Sarah was trying and she knew her father was trying, too.

When she got home, out of breath from running, he was in the kitchen making biscuits. When he caught sight of her, he began to sing an old sea chantey he loved:

When I was out walking on Paradise Street,
Heave Ho, blow the man down,
A pretty young maiden I chanced for to meet,
Give me some time to blow the man down.

Sarah was glad to hear her father singing. Before her mother died, he used to sing a lot, and joke and make up funny names for people. Sarahcadabra, Sarahdoodle, Sarahcakes for Sarah. Only her mother called her Star. It was almost a secret name because with teachers, or on the phone to Grandmother and Grandfather in Massachusetts, her mother called her Sarah. When they were alone, whispering goodnight, walking in the mountains, her mother called her Star.

Those were bright days, Sarah thought now. Days full of light. But Mama said that people's lives were made up of lights and darks like a photograph, sad and glad together, all part of the picture, all part of life.

"Want some help?" she asked.

"No way, kiddo," he said. "These are super-duper only-a-Dad-can-make-em biscuits. I'm making dinner for some very important people."

"Who's coming?"

"Gerald and Sarah Stewart."

"Oh, Dad!"

She smelled something good, grabbed a pot holder and lifted the lid of a big pot on the stove. Chili. Her favorite. There were salad greens in a wooden bowl on the counter.

"Pretty fancy, Dad," she said, and set the table with the prettiest place mats and went to her room to change her shirt and brush her hair. She brushed and brushed, not because her hair needed brushing but because she needed time to think. She was trying to decide. Should she tell him?

After supper she did. "I was up in the canyon today," she said, "with Mama."

"What?"

"Mama was with me."

"Are you saying you saw your mother in the canyon?"

"Not exactly. I was leaning on the flat rock with my feet in the water—the way I was when she took that photograph of me—and I could feel her hand touching my hair."

"Oh, Sarah," her father said, laying down his book and looking distressed. "Your mother was a very special person. She loved you very much. I want you to remember her always. As I will. But you can't bring her back. You have to accept that." He sighed. "Oh, dear," he said softly, almost to himself, "I thought letting you go to the canyon would help, would make it easier for you."

He held out his arms and she went into them. He hugged her tightly, his face twisted with pain. There were so many things she wanted to say but it was hurting him too much. She wanted to tell him that going to the canyon did help, that she couldn't bear it if she couldn't go. She wanted to talk to him about this feeling she had that she was supposed to be in the canyon, taking photographs, carrying on Mama's work. She had been doing that today and for the first time since Mama died her heart had stopped aching and she had been able to see clearly instead of through a kind of mist. She was sure that she had at least three good pictures—and that Mama knew and was pleased. The feeling was fading and she wanted to ask him how to hang on to it but he looked too sad.

So she said, "I'm okay Dad, really. I had a good time in the canyon today. There's tons of brittlebush in bloom. Look." She pointed to the legs of her jeans which were dusted with golden pollen. "It was like wading through sun."

Her father smiled. "As a boy, I liked to wade in the Atlantic Ocean when a storm was brewing. My mother was afraid I'd get swept out to sea. Parents are like that."

"I know," Sarah said. "But kids have to grow."

"So they do, Sarahcadabra," he said, ruffling her hair. "So they do."

She fell asleep happily planning a long walk in the canyon on Saturday. She would ask her father to go with her. They would find the second waterfall, stand under it, maybe swim in the deep pool below it. Being there, doing things they used to do when Mama was alive would make them a family again, calm and safe and happy. After all, the earth could never die.

At midnight, Sarah woke up screaming. Her mother lay deep in Magic Canyon, beside the stream. Her foot was in a trap, there was a hole in the sky, poison was dripping down on her and the water in the stream was rising fast and a boulder as big as a house tottered on the rim of the canyon ready to fall. "Mama! Mama! Mama!" Sarah screamed.

"Sarah, baby, what is it?" It was her father's voice. "Are you sick? What's the trouble?"

"It's Mama," Sarah cried. "She's going to be poisoned, drowned, crushed. We have to help her."

"No, no, sweetheart, Mama is dead. She can't be hurt by anyone or anything. Not anymore. Not ever."

"But I saw her. She was trapped and the water was rising and there was this boulder. It's going to fall."

"It was a dream, darling, that's all. Only a dream."

"But it was so real."

"I know, Sarah," her father said seriously. "Dreams often seem very real, but they're not. Honestly. Here." He handed her a tissue. She tried to wipe her eyes without moving her head out from under his hand. She wanted him to keep stroking her hair, to keep talking so the worried feeling would go away.

"I never had a dream this real in my whole life," she said. "It must mean something."

"It probably means that my cooking was giving you indigestion." He said it jokingly but he sat with her until she went back to sleep.

Sarah woke to a beautiful sunny day. She remembered her dream but it no longer seemed real. She dressed, ate breakfast and grabbed her jacket, pausing to empty its pockets onto the porch table. The roll of film she had used yesterday tumbled out, along with a half-eaten cookie, a spotted owl feather and a curiously shaped red stone she didn't remember picking up.

But picking up stones was something she did automatically whenever an interesting one caught her eye. There were stones all over the house. Sarah loved them for their color and shape and the way they felt in her hand. Her father was interested in how old they were and what they revealed about the way earth burned and cooled, cracked and shifted, wore away and built itself up over millions and millions of years. She put the red stone back in her pocket. When she got a chance she would look it up, identify it, find out whether it was born of fire or water or polar ice.

She went out and stood near the stop sign on the highway to wait for the school bus. Suddenly the cool-edged quiet of the morning was pierced by the siren of a fire truck screaming up the access road to the mountains. She followed the truck with her eyes and gasped when she saw that it was heading for a flickering orange dot of flame at the mouth of Magic Canyon.

The school bus pulled to a stop and its door swung open. "All aboard," the driver called cheerily. Sarah got on and walked quickly to the back of the bus where she could watch the orange dot through the rear window as the bus pulled away.

All day at school, Sarah worried about the canyon. She stared at her math workbook and saw towering Washingtonian palms, fluttery cottonwood trees, bunchgrass and staghorn cholla. Was the fire eating them up this very minute while she memorized multiplication tables? Had the fire been burning all night or had it just begun?

On the bus on the way home, Sarah sat on the edge of her seat, her forehead pressed against the glass of the window. Hurry, hurry, she whispered to the wheels. At her stop, she jumped off the bus and ran straight across the flat land that fanned out from the mouth of the canyon. Usually, she entered the canyon from above, but the ball of fire she had seen this morning had been on the desert floor.

What she saw took her breath away. The palms, the cottonwood trees, every single one, stood tall and safe and beautiful in the pale gold afternoon sun.

But there had been a fire, and it had eaten something up. A huge bulldozer had been reduced to a blackened piece of junk. What was a bulldozer doing here? She looked around and saw the unmistakable signs of a construction project. A row of stakes, with orange plastic ribbons tied to them, led into the canyon. She wanted to follow them but she was supposed to go straight home after school and she was late already. She turned and ran, arriving home breathless to tell her father what she had seen in the canyon.

It was on the six o'clock local television news. Charlie Night, a Cahuilla Indian, had been arrested. The charge was statutory arson and attempted murder. Allegedly, Mr. Night had burned up a bulldozer and terrorized the operator.

Willard Olefin, who worked for Valley Construction, Inc., said into the microphone that the reporter held out to him: "I thought I was losing my marbles. I was up there all alone, and all of a sudden this naked savage jumps out in front of me, and starts threatening me with a bow and arrow."

"What did you do?" the reporter asked.

"I took off."

The reporter laughed.

"It's no joke," Willard Olefin said, sulkily.

The newscaster said the incident had occurred in the early morning near Creation Mountain at the mouth of a small canyon where the Grandview Corporation was breaking ground for a multiuse complex that would include luxury homes, a hotel and an eighteen-hole golf course.

"In Magic Canyon?" Sarah gasped. She was standing behind her father's chair, staring over his shoulder at the television screen.

The newscaster was saying that Charles Night, wearing only a breechclout, leggings and beaded moccasins was found standing on a small hill near the mouth of the canyon. His arms were raised and he was looking up at the sky as if in prayer. A small bow and a quiver of obsidian-tipped arrows lay at his feet. He was apprehended without a struggle.

The screen showed the blackened bulldozer and the construction site, but the camera crew had arrived too late to get any pictures of Charlie Night. The television newscaster said Mr. Night's motives were unclear. Onlookers reported hearing him say that he was trying to save his mother's home.

But firefighters said that there were no houses in the canyon.

By seven the next morning, Sarah was dressed and had her bookbag packed. She took a bowl of cereal into the living room and turned on the television. The local news station reported another burglary in the Wellstown area and a tractor trailer accident on the highway.

"Why don't they tell about Magic Canyon?" Sarah exclaimed. "What's happening to Charlie Night?"

As if in answer to her question, the newscaster announced that the prominent trial lawyer, Steven Karloff, had arrived from Los Angeles last night to represent the Indian charged with arson and attempted murder. Bail of $25,000 had been set and posted and a meeting with Judge John Drummond was scheduled for today. In the airport, Mr. Karloff made a brief statement for the television cameras. He said that his client, Charles Night, was not guilty as charged. He had not attempted or threatened to kill anyone. His intentions were quite the opposite. He was trying to preserve life. A fragile ecosystem was in danger and Mr. Night was trying to protect it.

At school that day, all Sarah could think of was Magic Canyon and Charlie Night. But nobody seemed to be worried about either one. There were more exciting things in the news. A cat burglar was on the loose and a big film studio was going to shoot a movie in town.

At dinner that evening Sarah asked her father what was going to happen to Charlie Night. "Will he have to go to jail?"

"Hard to say, honey. He scared the daylights out of that bull-dozer operator but it's pretty clear he didn't mean him any harm. It was obviously a ceremonial act. He was making a protest. People have a right to protest—but not to build bonfires on other people's expensive machines."

Sarah insisted on watching the news at six and at eight and if her father had let her she would have stayed up to watch it at eleven. But there was no further mention of Charlie Night or Magic Canyon. "I can't believe it!" Sarah was outraged. "A person risks going to jail to save the most beautiful place in the world, and they just drop the story?"

"Nothing's deader than yesterday's news," her father said.

But by the next morning the story was alive again. Charlie was free. The judge had decided that there were no grounds for the accusation of attempted murder. The developer and the bulldozer operator had agreed not to press criminal charges if Mr. Night paid for work hours lost and damage to the bulldozer. The money had been paid by an organization called the Badger Society. And Mr. Night was standing ready to make a statement for the television audience.

As it turned out, Mr. Night was ready but the audio equipment was not. As a result, the television audience saw Charlie standing straight and silent while technicians bustled around. Sarah stared at the screen, fascinated.

Charlie Night was taller and thinner than most of the Indians she saw around town. His hair was black, the kind of shiny black that has blue and green lights in it when the sun shines on it. He didn't carry a bow and arrow, and he wore jeans, not leggings, running shoes, not moccasins, and a denim shirt with rolled up sleeves. He looked familiar. Charlie Night, Sarah realized with a start, looked like Hiawatha. Her father said that book illustrations and a lot of the ideas people had about Indians were stereotypes—false or only half true. He said that in real life Indians were short and tall, fat and thin, wise and foolish, kind and cruel like everybody else. Maybe so, Sarah thought, but Charlie looked like a picture in one of her favorite books. Under the picture, it said "Hiawatha, noble savage."

The bulldozer operator had called Charlie a savage. If he was, Sarah decided, he was a noble one. He was, after all, trying to save Magic Canyon.

Gerald Stewart's reaction to Charlie's appearance was also one of surprise. "Why, he's not much more than a boy," he said. "I guess I was expecting some aging hippie left over from the sixties."

"Don't shoot!" an electrician joked as he pulled a cable across Charlie's foot.

Charlie didn't look down. His gaze was fixed straight ahead as if he could see everyone in the television audience, as if he could see everyone in the world—as if he could see Sarah.

Speaking slowly in a low voice, he said: "I am Charlie Night, a child of the earth. We are all children of the earth. I would speak to you of our mother. I would ask you to remember her loving arms, the canyons that run up from the desert into the mountains of Arizona, New Mexico, California and Colorado.

"Here, ancient legends say, life began. And here since a time before memory, the children of earth have found food, water, shelter and beauty to make our hearts sing.

"Shall we cut off these loving arms? Break our mother's bones? Drain out her blood? What is important? Air quality? Oceans? Rain forests? A spotted owl? All, all are important. Because all are part of the circle of life. Remove any piece and we break the chain.

"What I did in Magic Canyon yesterday was unwise, a mistake for which I am sorry. But it was not hasty. For two years I have been working with my brothers and sisters, Indians and non-Indians, to save an endangered species—the magical canyons where our past and our futures lie.

"We have raised money, obtained legal counsel, made environmental impact studies. There have been meetings, letters, reports, documents filed. We are told to be patient, but time is running out. Our mother is in danger and because our mother is in danger, we are in danger.

"Whatever happens to a handful of river stones, happens to us all."

The station began broadcasting the weather forecast. Mr. Stewart turned the set off. "C'mon, honey," he said. "Time to go."

But Sarah just sat there. She couldn't believe it. Charlie's speech! Her mother, Abigail Stewart, could have made it. They had the same ideas, the same way of looking at things. Mama often said that she belonged to the earth, that we all do, that the earth is our mother. But until recently, Sarah hadn't given the matter much thought. She had been content to go to the canyon with Mama, explore its mysteries, marvel at its beauty, meet the birds and animals that lived there and come home tired and happy. Now that her mother was gone, the canyon seemed to be calling Sarah back, again and again, as if there were hidden meanings there she was meant to discover.

Her father drove Sarah to school and they talked about Magic Canyon and Charlie Night's protest. "I think they'll win," Sarah said. "Charlie and the people he's working with."

"I hope so," her father said, "but I wouldn't count on it. When it comes to environmentalists, they win some and they lose some, and in a case like this, where it's a place nobody knows about and there's nothing dramatic like the bald eagle to attract attention, they'll probably lose."

"But we can tell people."

"Yes, but it will be hard to get them to listen, much less agree."

At noon, Sarah saw what her father meant. She had planned to tell everyone in the lunchroom about the trees and flowers and birds and animals, about the water and the rocks and the cool, fragrant air that made Magic Canyon special. Then they could tell their parents and their parents could tell their friends. But the lunchroom was very noisy and the boys had folded their paper napkins into airplanes and were throwing them around. She didn't know how to get their attention, so she asked Consuela to help her get some of the girls together. When Consuela heard what Sarah wanted to talk about, her eyes widened dramatically. "Ooh," she said, "I think it's so scary having a wild Indian running around loose. What if he climbs in the window at night? What if he burns up the school bus?"

"Oh, Consuela," Sarah said disgustedly, "he's not going to burn up a school bus. He's trying to save the earth."

"That's his story," one of the boys said. By now, the boys had come over to see what the girls were arguing about. "What does saving one little canyon have to do with saving the earth? I think he's just jealous. My dad says that Indians who own land can sell it to a developer and make a lot of money. Charlie probably doesn't own any land and it's sort of like if I can't get rich, I don't want anybody else to."

Now everybody got into the discussion. "The developer can't just stop," an older boy said. "If somebody would buy his land for more than he paid for it, he might sell it. But that's not going to happen."

"Why not?" Sarah asked.

"Because it would cost a million dollars."

"More."

Sarah tried to get them to talk about the migrating birds who needed Magic Canyon as a rest stop along their way, about the dancing water that kept alive more wild creatures than even she had seen.

But the group was excited about the developer's plans. Condominiums. A scenic road with private homes on it running up to the top of the canyon. A four-story hotel, an eighteen-hole golf course, tennis courts.

Sarah's heart began to pound. Almost without knowing where she was or what she was doing, she climbed up on a chair, then on the table. "Stop it, stop it, stop it," she screamed. "You're talking about ruining a beautiful place, killing the mother of us all, the earth. Didn't you understand what Charlie Night was saying on television last night?"

"Indian Charlie?" a red-haired boy said. "Who cares what he says? Does he play golf?"

Suddenly everyone was laughing and Sarah was crying.

Horrified, she realized that she was standing on a lunchroom table with tears streaming down her cheeks. She got down and ran into the girls' room. She was leaning against the tile wall and sobbing when she felt a hand on her shoulder.

It was Consuela. "I'm sorry, I didn't mean to upset you. I was just being funny. So was Billy."

"I know," Sarah said. "I can't believe what I did. You must think I'm crazy."

"For yelling? In my family, everybody yells. Especially my mom."

At two o'clock, when the class went to the library, Sarah's teacher asked her to stay behind. "You were upset at lunch-time," she said. "The children said it was something about your mother."

Sarah said nothing.

The teacher waited. Sarah remained silent. Finally, the teacher said, "It's all right if you don't want to talk about it."

Again Sarah felt like screaming, because she did want to talk about it. She wanted to make wonderful speeches and make everybody see. But she wasn't good enough with words. She was better at drawing and hiking and recognizing sedimentary rock and making star charts. "May I go to the library now?" she asked.

"Of course, Sarah," the teacher said, "but please let me know if I can help."

Sarah nodded. How could she explain something she, herself, didn't understand: her dreams and the feeling that saving Magic Canyon was the most important thing in the world and that in some mystical way, she, Sarah Star Stewart, was being asked to do it.

She was glad her father was there when she got home. She just had to to tell him what had happened at lunch. But telling it brought her close to tears again. The noisy boys, the silly girls, everybody trying to talk at once and the horrible feeling she suddenly had that the kids were right in one way but they were seeing only tiny little pieces of a picture you could only understand if you saw the whole thing. And even she couldn't do that. "I failed," she told her father, miserably.

He touched her shoulder gently. "You did your best. That's all anyone can do. Besides," he said, picking up the paper, "the ball game may not be over yet. Look at this."

On the first page of the inside section of the newspaper, there were two articles relating to Magic Canyon. One was an interview with the developer who said that the condos and the hotel would be limited to four stories and made of natural stone to blend in with the canyon walls. The waters of the canyon would be diverted into a concrete canal that would wind gracefully through the golf course and be beautified on both sides with planters filled with brightly colored flowers. All told, what was being done would have limited impact on the environment because the only endangered species known to inhabit the canyon was a small bird called the least Bell's vireo and none had been seen for the past two years. A lot of people were quoted saying the development would create jobs and be good for the local economy. It was progress and you can't stop progress. They sounded like the kids in school.

The other article was about the Badger Society, an organization working to protect the unique ecology and sacred spirit of
desert canyons. In the group were medicine men, healers and
seers. They had come from all over, from Arizona, Colorado,
New Mexico, Nevada, to fast and pray for a small canyon almost unknown until it figured in yesterday's news. William
Songchanter, a holy man of the Sioux, who was almost one
hundred years old and well known for his wisdom, was a
member. So was Charlie Night.

"Funny name for an organization," Sarah's father said. "I
wonder why they chose a badger instead of something grander
like a grizzly bear or a mountain lion."

"Because the badger is an Indian medicine man," Sarah said.

"He knows which roots are good for healing and he shows people where to find them. Mama says there really are roots that work like medicine and badgers do a lot of digging. So if you need a medicine root, just follow a badger path. Once when I had a cough, Mama gave me a piece of a root the Indians call bear root. She told me to suck on it like a cough drop. She said Navajo singers use it to soothe their throats when they sing all night."

Smiling, Sarah told her father about Sneaky, a big black badger that lived near Cougar Rock at the foot of Magic Canyon. Badgers were supposed to come out only after dark but Sneaky was a character. He loved to dig and he'd do it night and day. Once Sarah was able to get close to his hole and watch. She got showered with sand as he backed out kicking earth and pebbles away with his back feet.

"*Ligusticum porter*," Gerald Stewart said.

"What?"

"The botanical name for bear root. Also called Osha. Did it cure your cough?"

"Yes," Sarah said.

"Interesting," Mr. Stewart said exactly as Sarah knew he would. Things that worked always interested him.

It was her favorite time and place, sunrise at the mouth of the canyon, the start of the magic. Everything was rose colored, the sandy earth of the desert floor, clusters of barrel and cholla cactus, clumps of brittlebush, the boulders in the wash that were older than time, the top ridge of the Wisdom Seekers mountain range, holding back the day. Sarah laid her face against Cougar Rock and imagined she heard the heartbeat of the universe.

Suddenly the peace was shattered by the screech of metal on stone, the growl of a motor, ripping, the grinding thud of tractor treads. Four large bulldozers were bearing down on her, one from each direction. Their gigantic steel blades were crushing, battering, destroying the earth. Gravel, rocks and even boulders were swept aside like so much litter. Insects and birds exploded into the air and small animals raced to and fro in terror, trying to protect their nests and young.

Sarah opened her mouth but no sound came out. Again and again she tried to scream, watching in horror until the churning blades of the bulldozers were upon her, about to slice her in half. Then suddenly she saw that it was not she, Sarah, who was huddled against Cougar Rock. It was her mother.

Sarah woke up shivering, although it was almost eight o'clock and the sun was spilling like warm honey over the windowsill onto the bedroom rug. She put her hand over her mouth in case the screams she had tried to get out in her dream decided to come out now. She did not want to startle her father who was in the kitchen making breakfast. She wanted to listen to the familiar scrape of the spoon against the pot as he stirred

[36]

the oatmeal, the squeak of the refrigerator door, the clunk of the toast jumping up and sometimes out of the toaster. She wanted to look around the room and run her fingers over the stitching of the patchwork quilt Grandma Stewart had made for her. She wanted to see and hear and touch the familiar world that had nothing to do with dreams.

She dressed and ate breakfast, saying nothing about her dream, determined to forget it, but as she waited for the school bus, her eyes went to the base of Creation Mountain where she saw a puff of smoke. Or was it dust? Suddenly, she was running as fast as she could toward Magic Canyon.

Four bulldozers were at work. They were not as big as the ones in her dream but in their mechanized power and steel armor, they were terrifying to someone on foot, someone eleven years old and small for her age. To do good, her mother said, it is necessary to be brave. Sarah said it to herself now, as she often did, chanting it like a little song. Do good. Be brave.

She ran up to the nearest bulldozer, which was about to push over Cougar Rock. Shouting and waving her arms, she tried to make the driver stop. The machine was making too much noise for the driver to hear but when he caught sight of Sarah's small frantic figure, he turned the engine off at once and climbed down. Sarah ran up to him, still shouting, "Stop, stop, you have to stop!"

A big man in a plaid shirt looked down on her, puzzled and concerned.

"What's the matter?" he asked and Sarah fought back tears because everything was the matter but looking at his face she knew that none of it would make sense to him if she told it to him in pieces. But that was the only way you could tell it. He was hurting her mother, he was crushing lizards, he was imprisoning water, tearing up Badger's home. The mountains were being scarred, ancient messages painted on rocks were being erased and the earth's life force was being drained away out of a thousand wounds like this one.

"You are damaging the planet," she said firmly. If the language of the heart could not prevail, she would try scientific words. "This canyon," she said, "is part of a very important, very fragile ecosystem."

"Aha," the driver said, "you're one of those. A greenie. An environmentalist. Well, that's nice, but I haven't got time to talk about it now. I've got work to do." He turned and walked back to his machine. Sarah followed and grabbed his sleeve. "Look, kid," he said, pulling away. "You can't hang around here. You'll get hurt."

Sarah stationed herself in front of the steel blade of the bulldozer with her arms stretched out. In the end, the driver had to summon the construction supervisor who called the sheriff who sent a young deputy out. Sarah refused to speak to any of them. There was nothing to say. She would not tell them her name or where she lived because she was not ready to go home, not ready to give up. She needed to think. She needed a plan.

She was glad that the sheriff was out when they got to his office. The deputy told her to sit in the waiting room. His office was across the way. He said that if she needed anything, she should let him know. He found a coloring book and some crayons which he gave to her. She did not tell him that she was too old for coloring books.

The waiting room was cool and dark. The bench was hard. The only sound was the ticking of a clock on the wall. It was a good place to think but she wasn't getting anywhere. Why couldn't she explain that Magic Canyon was as important as Grand Canyon, that a leaf-nosed bat was as important as a golden eagle, because they were all connected—to each other and to everything else. She had thought it was because she couldn't find the right words, but Charlie Night had made a beautiful speech and all that the kids at school could remember was that he'd built a fire on top of a bulldozer. What if she could take the whole class to Magic Canyon, show them the hidden cave, the cactus wren's nest, the rock paintings? Would they understand? Probably not. Consuela was afraid of lizards and Billy Parker would bring along his Walkman.

What could she do? Her mother used to say, "Follow your dreams," but how could she if she didn't know what her dreams meant?

"Mind if I join you?" A man with a beard and bright blue eyes, wearing rumpled chinos, had come in and was standing at her elbow.

"Okay," she said.

The man sat down on the bench beside her. "Waiting for the sheriff?"

Sarah nodded.

"Me, too. My name is Cornelius Blake but everybody calls me Corey."

Sarah said nothing.

"I'm a reporter," Corey said. Again he waited for a reply. After a while he said, "Are you?"

"Am I what?"

"A reporter."

She had been worrying so long and it was such a silly question, Sarah found herself laughing. "No," she said, "I'm a failure."

"What have you failed at?"

"Well, most recently I tried to stop a bulldozer."

"What? You, too? What is it with you people? Do you all hate bulldozers? Are they about to become an endangered species? I just heard about a guy who lighted a fire on one. I'm supposed to do an interview with him for my magazine. But I think there's a bigger story here. Or right around the corner. A story that will knock your socks off. Sometimes something that seems insignificant—like this little, out-of-the-way canyon—turns out to be the tip of the iceberg, so to speak. A major news event. You never know."

"This person who burned the bulldozer," Sarah said, "was his name Charlie Night?"

"Yes. Are you a friend of his?"

"No, but I'd like to be," Sarah said.

"I think I'd like him for a friend, too," Corey Blake said, and went on, talking more to himself than to Sarah. "He sounds like an interesting guy. He has a degree in geology and works as a field researcher on various projects for earth science organizations. He appears to be a pretty good scientist and a dedicated environmentalist but he told me that his scientific studies have convinced him that research and technology alone are not going to be able to save the earth. And so—probably because his mother was a Cahuilla medicine woman—he has begun to explore old wisdom, old magic—attitudes and beliefs that inspired his Indian ancestors to live on the earth without wrecking it. I guess what impresses me most is that William Songchanter has chosen to be this young Indian's spiritual teacher."

"Who's William Songchanter?" Sarah asked, fascinated by what she was hearing.

"Good question. Nobody I know has ever seen him. But everyone I talk to knows who he is—a holy man and ceremonial chief of the Teton Sioux, a seer, a teacher, a healer. He's supposed to be one hundred years old. Yet he seems to be the active force behind a powerful Indian organization called the Badger Society."

"What is the holy man teaching Charlie?"

"Oh, ancient ceremonies, the meaning of dreams—things like that."

"Charlie can tell people what their dreams mean?"

"I don't know. In fact, I don't know a heck of a lot about any of this stuff. But Charlie Night has aroused my curiosity. That's why I'm chasing him. I want to learn more. But first I need to learn where I can find him. I thought the sheriff might give me a clue. Unfortunately, I can't hang around here any longer. I'm already late for a meeting with a developer."

Sarah glared.

"Why the face?"

"I hate developers."

"Well, this one's a nice guy. Honest. He didn't force anybody to sell their land to him and he paid a good price for it. What he's planning to build looks pretty good, too. No skyscrapers, just a four-story hotel at the base of the canyon and individual homes along a winding road up the mountain. He says he'll do a lot of planting. They always say that but I believe this guy."

"I suppose you think bulldozers are nice, too," Sarah said, sarcastically.

"Actually, I do. Up there in the driver's seat, you feel like king of the mountain. You ought to try it some time. It's fun. Well, gotta run. I enjoyed talking to you, whoever you are."

Before Sarah could say anything, Corey Blake had grabbed up his camera bag and was out the door. He was, Sarah thought, an exasperating person. But talking to him had made her feel better. It had also given her an idea. If she could find Charlie Night, he might be able to tell her what her dreams meant.

It was almost five before the sheriff arrived. "I hear you've been trying to stop a bulldozer," he said.

"Yes, sir."

"Well, if you were trying to attract attention to Magic Canyon you could have saved yourself the trouble. The mayor and council have been in session all afternoon, considering a petition for the city to acquire the canyon by right of eminent domain and preserve it as a wilderness area."

"What's eminent domain?" Sarah asked.

"Taking private land for public use."

"Without paying for it?"

"No, the city would have to pay."

"What if the owner won't sell?"

"He has to."

"That's the law?" Sarah wanted to know.

"The law and the Fifth Amendment to the United States Constitution," the sheriff said.

"Are they going to do it?" Sarah asked. "Buy the canyon and keep it wild?"

"I doubt it," the sheriff said. "But they agreed to hold a public hearing on it in September. Until then, the developer can't turn a stone up there. Of course, the tree huggers and pot hunters can make more studies, try to turn up a piece of pottery or a thigh bone or a bighorn sheep. Ever see a bighorn up there?"

"No," Sarah said, "but my mother did."

"Well, maybe they'll ask her to testify at the hearing."

"She can't," Sarah said. "She's dead."

"Oh," the sheriff said, looking down at his hands. "I'm sorry. But you can stop worrying about the canyon for a nice long while. Go play there. Have fun. Things will work out. Now," he said looking up, "how about telling me your name and letting me call your Dad or whoever takes care of you so he can come and take you home?"

When her father walked into the room Sarah ran to him. He hugged her and drove home with his arm around her. She fell asleep on the way, her face against the pens and pencils in his jacket pocket.

When they got home they microwaved a pizza and ate almost in silence. Her father seemed to be waiting for her to say something, but what was there to say? The sheriff had told him what she had done. What she really wanted to talk about was the hearing and how they could get the city to buy Magic Canyon and keep it wild. But she had a feeling it would not be a good idea. Her father looked as if something were weighing on his mind.

"Sarah," he said, when they had finished eating, "this really has to stop. Yesterday your teacher telephoned. She told me she was worried about you. She said you got up on a lunchroom table and shouted. I can't believe you would do a thing like that. And today, the sheriff phoned to tell me you'd been hauled in for trying to stop a bulldozer."

"I'm sorry, Daddy," Sarah said. "It was a stupid thing to do."

"It's worse than that. If you were an adult, they could arrest you for trespassing. I'm also disappointed because you weren't being honest with me—pretending you were going to school and then going to the construction site instead."

"I meant to go to school. I was waiting for the bus. But last night I had this dream, this awful dream." She tried to tell him about the bulldozers that were going to cut her in half, only it was Mama, and how she had to try to stop them but she couldn't get the words out because the horror of the dream was choking her.

"Take it easy, sweetheart," her father said, looking at her in an odd way—as if *he* were frightened. "I know you were only trying to do what you thought was right. But I can see that it's all becoming too much for you. We'll have to think of some way to make it easier on you, take your mind off it for a while, a change of scene, maybe. But don't you worry about it. I'll think of something."

Then, briskly, as if he were the one with the bad dream and were shaking it off, he said, "Well, what shall we do now? Shall we play a game?"

After dinner, he usually read the newspaper. She knew he enjoyed it and she was touched that he would offer to play a game with her instead. But it wasn't necessary. In fact, she wanted them to slip back into their usual, comforting routine.

"I was thinking of working on my star chart."

"Astronomy is fascinating, isn't it?" her father said, looking relieved. "Would you like to use your grandfather's book?"

"Yes, please."

She loved the large, leatherbound volume with its foldout maps of the heavens. Propping it open on the desk, she stared at the clouds of stars in the Milky Way. Wouldn't it be wonderful, she thought, to be a real star, with an assigned place in the galaxy? To be part of a constellation. To be needed as part of something that was part of everything, the way the three stars in the Big Dipper were needed to form the tail of Ursa Major, the Great Bear in the sky.

"You know, honey," Gerald Stewart said to his daughter that night as they were putting away the beautiful astrology book, "nobody expects you to save the world."

But Mama would try, Sarah thought later as she lay in bed, her head full of questions about the canyon: Would the archaeologists find sacred objects? Would the naturalists find big horn sheep? How many sacred objects and how many sheep would have to be found to save Magic Canyon? She was beginning to get angry at the way the law worked. She was also beginning to get angry with herself. She was doing too much worrying and too much talking. Worrying didn't help and she wasn't getting anywhere with words. There had to be something she could do. If only she could talk to her mother. Mama would understand. She would help her, would tell her what to do.

Sarah stared at the patch of desert sky framed by her bedroom window. It was strewn with stars, one brighter than the rest. A wishing star? She knew wishing on a star didn't make wishes come true, but she stared at the star as hard as she could.

She had no idea how long she stared at that star. A minute or an hour. But the next thing she knew she was in Magic Canyon with Mama and Mama was singing, "Will you, won't you, will you, won't you come and dance with me?" and then they were dancing, Sarah and Mama, dancing a coyote dance, a badger dance, a spotted fawn, porcupine, gopher snake, woodpecker, butterfly, chuckwalla, hummingbird dance, and all the birds and animals, lizards and snakes in the canyon had gathered to watch, knowing that the dancing was for them, to honor them.

[44]

Finally the dance was done and the wild creatures began to slip away. Mama kissed Sarah lightly on the forehead. "Follow Badger," she whispered. Sarah turned to see where Badger was going and when she turned back Mama was gone.

Badger, however, was still in sight, moving along quickly and purposefully in a series of short trots, stopping at frequent intervals to cock his head and listen. Was he expecting to be followed? Waiting for her? Sarah hoped so because she knew from experience that if a badger didn't want to be followed, he knew a dozen ways to disappear. And it was no good staking out the entrance to his home. He'd have other ways of getting in and out. Badger was not only a medicine man, he was an architect. He constructed whole cities underground. And if he suddenly wanted a hole to hide in he could dig one in less than two minutes.

It was late afternoon. Violet shadows filled the canyon. Still, as long as the badger trotted along the stream, his webbed front feet sometimes sloshing in the water, it was easy for Sarah to keep him in sight, and even when it got darker, the streak of white fur on the animal's wedge-shaped head pointed the way like an arrow. Suddenly there was no white streak. No badger. And although Sarah was familiar with the tricky ways of badgers, she was disappointed and dismayed. What was she supposed to do now? She had kept her eyes fixed on that white stripe and now she didn't even know where she was.

Gradually, her eyes became accustomed to the dark and she recognized the huge column of rock directly in front of her. It was one of Magic Canyon's most striking features. Almost seven feet tall, carved and polished by the wind, it resembled a soldier or an Indian standing watch. Now that she was close enough to touch it, Sarah could see that it was definitely an Indian, standing straight as a lodgepole pine but with the face of a very old man. He wore a buffalo robe painted with stars and a necklace of bear claws. A hummingbird perched on his left shoulder. "Welcome, Star," the Indian said. "We have been expecting you."

Peering into the darkness, Sarah saw that all the creatures of the canyon had gathered in a circle, their eyes like points of green fire in the darkness.

The Indian raised his right hand. On his index finger, Sarah saw a ring set with a red stone in the shape of a turtle. "What is your heart's desire?" the Indian asked.

"I want to help my mother," Sarah answered. "She's part of the earth now and the earth is being destroyed."

"Your desire is worthy," the Indian said. "I will show you the way."

Then one by one, in twos and threes, sometimes in a flurry like snowflakes, pictures appeared and disappeared to make way for new ones. It was like a slide show or a movie and it was telling a story, a story about a journey Sarah had to make to save Magic Canyon and help heal the earth. The pictures were like a road map. They were also the reason for the journey. Sarah was supposed to take photographs the way Mama did to make people love the earth so much they couldn't bear to hurt it.

When the last picture faded, Sarah looked up. The Indian had turned to stone and the animals had gone—except for the hummingbird which hovered over something on the path. Sarah bent to look. A red stone. She picked it up and turned to look for the bird but there was no sign of it and the mountain was flooded with dawn.

When she woke up, Sarah felt calm and happy. She had a mission. She knew what she was supposed to do and felt sure she could do it. After all, she had Mama's camera and Mama had taught her how to use it. And she was delighted to find that she could recall all the pictures she had seen in her dream. The secret cave in Magic Canyon, cliff roses, a red rock mesa shaped like a ship, a silvery fish, petroglyphs. She could hold the pictures up in her mind, study them, put them down and then go back to them for another look. Good, she thought, that will be useful on my journey. She still did not know where she was supposed to go but she would figure it out. The pictures were clues. She would investigate them. Like a detective.

At noon, Sarah went to the school library. She studied a tourist guide to the Southwest, looked through bird and flower guides and pored over a book called *Tracking and Desert Survival*. Reluctantly she put it back on the shelf. Lunchtime was almost over and she needed to know more about the ancients who lived in cliff houses, used wild plants for food and medicine, knew the language of the animals and could move in and out of the spirit world like music or the scent of sage.

Confronted with row upon row of books, many of them with beautiful illustrations, Sarah didn't know where to begin. Inexplicably her hand went to a rather plain-looking book called *Desert Whispers*. Leafing through it, she found it was a collection of the wisdom and vision of Native Americans told in their own words.

No pictures. Just words floating on the page. She began to read where the book fell open:

Do not be afraid of dreams or memories.
The unknown is our native land.
The unseen is our element as much as air.
When a feather of curiosity falls, look up.
The bird of truth may be there.

How strange, Sarah thought, looking to see who had written the haunting words. A note at the bottom of the page credited Cahuilla medicine woman Gladys Hummingbird: "Noted for her ability to heal the body with natural remedies, Gladys Hummingbird also ministered to the mind and spirit of her patients by sharing ancient wisdom and insights. She died at ninety-two. Her daughter Gladys Night is carrying on her work. Mrs. Night's Indian name is Hummingbird Speaking."

At home that afternoon, Sarah took out the area phone book. There were eleven Nights, none with Charles for a first or middle name. She could call them all but there must be a simpler way. The sheriff might know where Charlie Night was but he wouldn't tell someone who was already giving him a hard time about Magic Canyon. If Corey Blake, the reporter knew, he would probably tell her. The trouble was, she didn't know where Corey Blake was. He had not mentioned the name of the news magazine he worked for. Well, how many news magazines were there? *Time, Life, Newsview, Newsweek.* Her father got most of them. She went to the pile of magazines on the porch. There it was on the masthead page of *Newsview*. Cornelius S. Blake. She telephoned *Newsview* and got the city desk. When she asked for Corey she was told that he was out west. She left her phone number and a message on his machine. "My name is Sarah Stewart. I'm the girl who tried to stop the bulldozer in Magic Canyon. I need to talk to you."

The phone rang while they were at dinner. Her father answered. "For you, Sarah," he said. "Fellow says he's Corey Blake." She flew past him to pick up the phone.

"Corey?"

"None other."

"You called."

"Reporters always call. What's up, kid?"

"Did you find Charlie Night?"

"Yes. I had a long talk with him. He got me so interested, I'm doing a piece on this idea of living in harmony with the earth. It's got me running all over the Southwest interviewing members of the Badger Society. So what can I do for you?"

"Tell me where Charlie lives."

"I'll be glad to, but he's not home. He's somewhere in the mountains on a vision quest, fasting and praying for wisdom and direction. Why are you looking for Charlie?"

"Well, it's kind of complicated, but I was hoping he could help me with a difficult journey I'm about to take."

Corey laughed. "I'm afraid Charlie's got a lot on his mind at the moment but anybody who can stand up to a bulldozer should be able to cope with a difficult journey. I wish you luck. Take care now."

"What was that about?" Sarah's father asked when she got back to the table. "You said something about taking a journey."

"Yes," she said, "I had a dream."

"Oh, no," her father groaned. "Not again."

"But this was a wonderful dream," she said and began to tell him about it. She told him about dancing with Mama in the canyon, about Badger turning into an Indian, about the journey she was supposed to take. "I'm supposed to photograph sacred places. Not just Magic Canyon, but other places that are in danger—places Mama told me about. I know the way and I'll recognize the places when I see them but they're far and I can't drive. If you would drive me, we could probably do it in a weekend. If we drove at night. And if I had to take a day off from school, it would be worth it."

Gerald Stewart put his cup down so suddenly that the coffee sloshed over the rim into the saucer. "Whoa!" he said. "Hold it right there. This dream stuff is getting out of hand. You're too old for fairy tales and make-believe."

"But," Sarah began.

"No buts," her father said. "We live in the real world whether we like it or not and that's all there is to it."

Then, in a gentler voice, he said he had something to tell her, something nice. He hadn't told her about it before because he was working out the details. But it was all set now. She would leave on the day after tomorrow for a long visit with Grandma and Grandpa Stewart on Cape Cod. School vacation was only two weeks away and he had arranged for her to get out early. He would put her on the plane and her grandparents would meet her in Boston. And when his teaching session closed, he'd join them. She would do all the wonderful things he had done when he was her age. She'd learn to launch a small boat, row, go sailing. She'd pick beach plums, dig for clams.

The day after tomorrow, Sarah gasped. She had to do something quick!

Lying in bed with the light off and her eyes wide open, her heart beating wildly, she waited until she could be sure her father was asleep. Then she slid out of bed and without turning on the light dressed quickly in the clothes she had laid out. She reached under her bed and pulled out her mother's camera, the light meter and four rolls of film. Then she reached back under the bed and brought out a coffee can that held her life's savings: four twenty-dollar bills and hundreds of pennies. The pennies might add up to as much as five dollars but they would be too heavy to take along and they might make noise when it was important to be quiet. She put the twenties in her shirt pocket and slid the can of pennies back under the bed.

She had already written the note. Actually, she had written three notes. In the first, she had tried to explain but it was too complicated so she tore that note up. Then she had printed a little sign that said "Gone to Arizona. Back soon." But that looked angry and rude. Finally she had copied a sample letter she found in a book.

Dear Dad:
Thank you and Grandma and Grandpa Stewart for inviting me to Cape Cod. I am sorry I cannot accept because I have a previous engagement. I have to save the canyon. (That's what Mama would do!)
                                        Sincerely,
                                        Sarah Star Stewart

At the bottom of the page, she put a long line of Xs.

She placed the note on the kitchen table, and made a couple of peanut butter sandwiches. She put them in her pack along with everything else she thought she might need on her journey. She put the pack on and, carrying her boots, eased the door open and stepped outside. She was carrying a flashlight but she was surprised at how well she could see without using it. She put her boots on and headed for Creation Mountain, black against a blue-black sky.

In the canyon it was harder to see and she turned the flashlight on. She wanted to save the batteries but she didn't want to fall into the water. An hour later, she was at the creek, taking her boots off and rolling up her jeans. The only way to enter the secret cave was to wade up a narrow side stream and duck around a waterfall that hid the entrance. That's what made the cave secret. You could walk right by it and never know it was there. She would be safe in the cave. Even if they hunted her with dogs, the dogs would lose the scent where she entered the water.

There were two parts to the cave. The first part was a rock shelf overlooking the small underground pool behind the waterfall. If you climbed through a vertical crack in the back wall, you would come into a vast cavern that Sarah and her

mother had only partially explored. Fresh air came in from several directions so the cave probably had other openings. She
hoped the openings were small—too small for a dog to get
through. Well, she couldn't worry about everything and by
tomorrow she would be gone.

Her plan was to hide here until early morning when she would slip out of the canyon and hike to Pine Crest, a little ski town where there was a Blue Line bus station. It was risky, but with luck, her father wouldn't find her note until eight or eight-thirty and there was a bus at ten-fifteen. She hoped eighty dollars was enough for a ticket.

When Sarah climbed out of the water onto what she and Mama called the front porch of their secret cave, her feet were numb with cold. She dried them with her sweater, rubbed them until the feeling came back and put her boots on again. The waterfall glistened with a hint of starlight, but behind it everything was dim and shadowy. It would be pitch-black in the big cavern, and she knew that was where she ought to sleep. If she stayed where she was, she might accidentally roll into the water. In the big cave, she could make noise, even light a fire with-out attracting attention. But she had noth-ing to make a fire with. She should have gathered palm fronds, dry grass and twigs on the way. Well, she wasn't about to wade back through that icy water to get some.

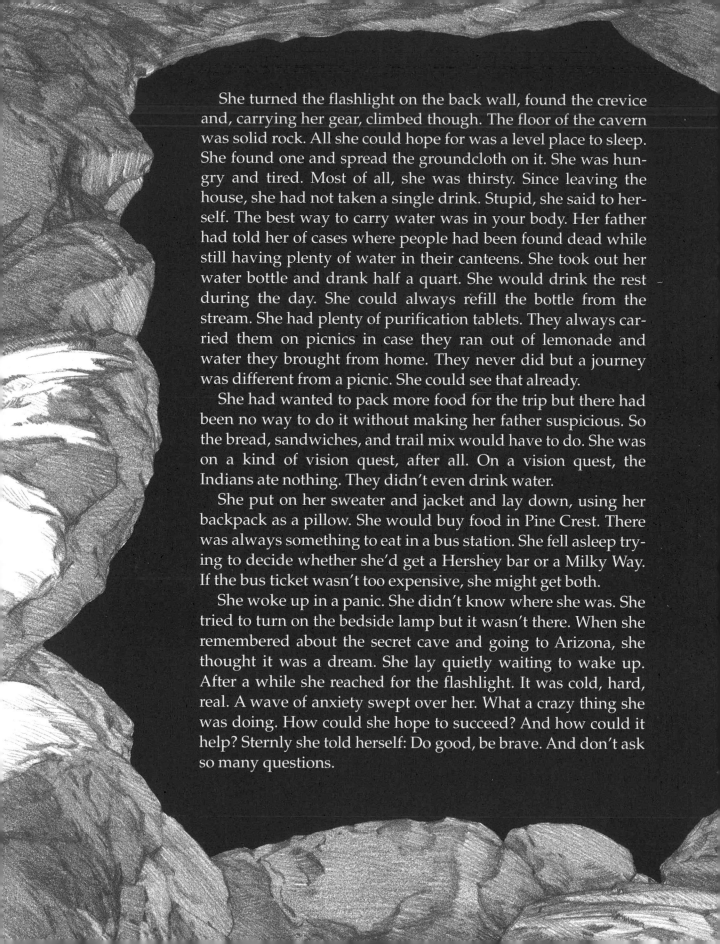

She turned the flashlight on the back wall, found the crevice and, carrying her gear, climbed though. The floor of the cavern was solid rock. All she could hope for was a level place to sleep. She found one and spread the groundcloth on it. She was hungry and tired. Most of all, she was thirsty. Since leaving the house, she had not taken a single drink. Stupid, she said to herself. The best way to carry water was in your body. Her father had told her of cases where people had been found dead while still having plenty of water in their canteens. She took out her water bottle and drank half a quart. She would drink the rest during the day. She could always refill the bottle from the stream. She had plenty of purification tablets. They always carried them on picnics in case they ran out of lemonade and water they brought from home. They never did but a journey was different from a picnic. She could see that already.

She had wanted to pack more food for the trip but there had been no way to do it without making her father suspicious. So the bread, sandwiches, and trail mix would have to do. She was on a kind of vision quest, after all. On a vision quest, the Indians ate nothing. They didn't even drink water.

She put on her sweater and jacket and lay down, using her backpack as a pillow. She would buy food in Pine Crest. There was always something to eat in a bus station. She fell asleep trying to decide whether she'd get a Hershey bar or a Milky Way. If the bus ticket wasn't too expensive, she might get both.

She woke up in a panic. She didn't know where she was. She tried to turn on the bedside lamp but it wasn't there. When she remembered about the secret cave and going to Arizona, she thought it was a dream. She lay quietly waiting to wake up. After a while she reached for the flashlight. It was cold, hard, real. A wave of anxiety swept over her. What a crazy thing she was doing. How could she hope to succeed? And how could it help? Sternly she told herself: Do good, be brave. And don't ask so many questions.

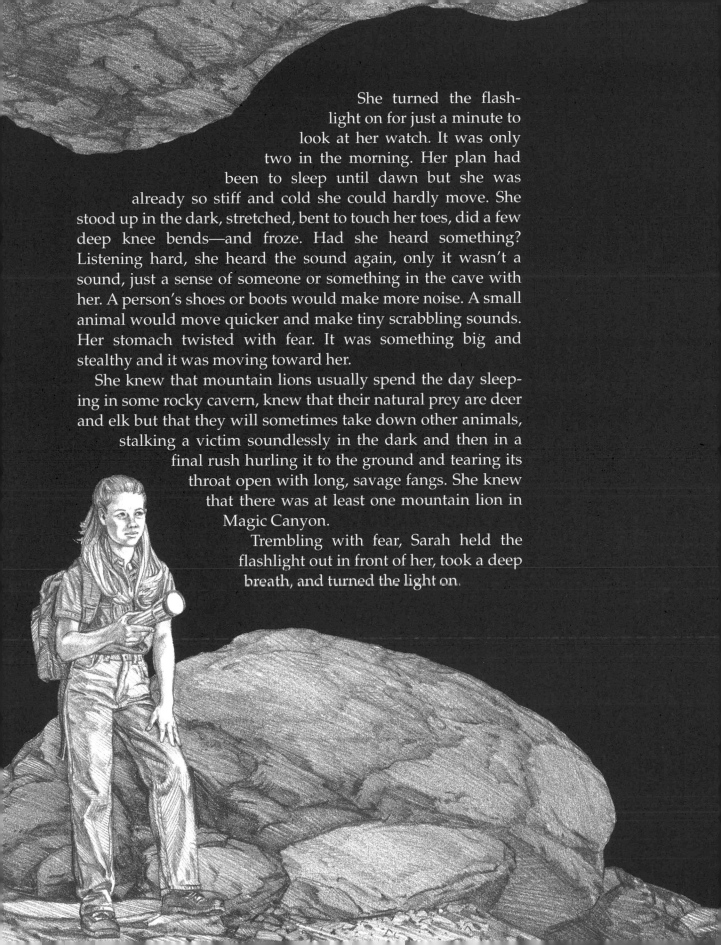

She turned the flash-
light on for just a minute to
look at her watch. It was only
two in the morning. Her plan had
been to sleep until dawn but she was
already so stiff and cold she could hardly move. She
stood up in the dark, stretched, bent to touch her toes, did a few
deep knee bends—and froze. Had she heard something?
Listening hard, she heard the sound again, only it wasn't a
sound, just a sense of someone or something in the cave with
her. A person's shoes or boots would make more noise. A small
animal would move quicker and make tiny scrabbling sounds.
Her stomach twisted with fear. It was something big and
stealthy and it was moving toward her.

She knew that mountain lions usually spend the day sleeping in some rocky cavern, knew that their natural prey are deer
and elk but that they will sometimes take down other animals,
stalking a victim soundlessly in the dark and then in a
final rush hurling it to the ground and tearing its
throat open with long, savage fangs. She knew
that there was at least one mountain lion in
Magic Canyon.

Trembling with fear, Sarah held the
flashlight out in front of her, took a deep
breath, and turned the light on.

•5•

"Charlie Night," Sarah gasped.

He was wearing beaded moccasins, a breechclout and leggings, and a beaded suede shirt with fringe. He carried a leather bag decorated with porcupine quills. He looked startled.

"What are you doing here?" Sarah asked. "Did my father send you?"

"No. Who is your father?"

"Gerald Stewart."

"I don't know him. And I'm sorry but I can't seem to remember meeting you."

"I'm Sarah Stewart and I have been looking for you."

"Why?"

"Because I want you to go with me on a difficult and dangerous journey." Charlie Night was looking puzzled.

"Where are your people?" he asked.

"What people?"

"The people you came here with."

"I came here alone. I'm on a long journey and this is the beginning of it. I'm going to Arizona and maybe Utah and Colorado."

From the look on Charlie's face Sarah knew that a storm of questions would follow, and they did. How old was she? Where were her parents? Didn't she know they'd be frantic? Didn't she know that it was dangerous for a little girl to be wandering around at night alone? In the canyon, okay, but in cities and on highways, terrible things happened. Didn't she

read the newspapers? Didn't she know that she must go back home right away?

Yes, yes, she knew. But there was something she had to do or the life would be drained out of Magic Canyon, the earth would suffer and Mama's spirit would grieve.

"Hey," Charlie said. "Don't look so sad. It's not that bad."

But it was, Sarah thought. Charlie was her last chance, her last hope. Her dream would die because nobody would listen.

"I'm listening," Charlie said quietly. "But I can't understand you if you cry."

Sarah wiped her eyes with her shirtsleeve. She was cold, shivering.

"I think you need a fire," Charlie said, gathering dry leaves and grass from the floor of the cave. Sarah took a tin container of matches from her backpack and handed it to him. "Okay," he said. "To save time, we could use these. But you should learn how to make a fire without matches. Do you know what a hearth board is?"

"Sure. My mother taught me how to make one, but I'm not very good at it."

Charlie took out a pointed stick and a flat board with a hole in it. He put a bit of dry grass under the hole and twirled the stick between his palms, arching his hands out stiffly, holding the board down with one knee. As black dust formed he

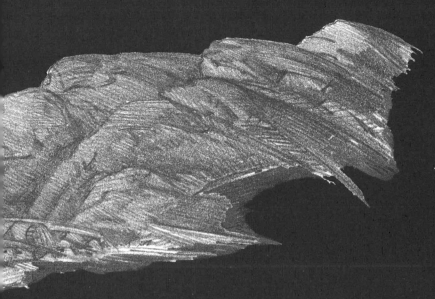

pushed it into the hole. When at last a curl of smoke appeared, he blew on it and fanned it with his hands until a tongue of bright gold flame leaped up.

"Neat," Sarah marveled, helping Charlie feed the flame with larger and larger twigs until they had a fire large enough to warm the cave and send shadows dancing on the walls. Slowly, as her body grew warm, her mind and heart became clear and calm. She knew she was here because Mother Earth needed the help of all of her children—the teeth of the wolf, the talons of the eagle, the stealth of the weasel, the sweetness of the evening primrose, the dreams and determination of Sarah Star Stewart.

Unzipping her backpack, she rummaged around for the half loaf of bread she had grabbed from the kitchen table on her way out. "We can make toast and I brought tea but I forgot to bring a pot or anything to boil water in." Charlie got to his feet, looked around the cave, disappeared for a few minutes and returned with an old basket that someone had evidently left behind.

"This should do the trick," he said, opening Sarah's water bottle and pouring water into the basket.

Sarah gasped. What sort of person would try to boil water in a basket? She held her breath, waiting for the water to run out. But it didn't. The basket was so tightly woven that not a drop seeped through. Was Charlie a magician?

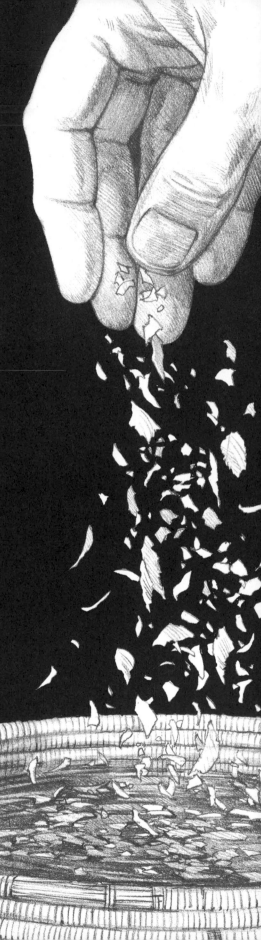

"Not really," he said. "This is a Cahuilla Indian basket. The Cahuilla are famous for weaving—hammocks, ropes, mats and beautiful baskets so tightly woven they can be used to carry water or flour or the tiniest of seeds. My grandmother wove baskets like this. Her name was Hummingbird."

"I know. I just read about her in a library book. She knew how to heal people with plants and herbs and knew the language of animals and birds."

"Right on," Charlie said. "You're a wise little owl."

"I'm not an owl," Sarah said, standing up with her arms out-stretched. "Guess what?"

"I guess you're a hummingbird moving your wings so fast it looks as if they're not moving at all."

"No fair! Your grandmother told you the answer," she said, faking a frown.

"Nope. My mother. Her Indian name was Hummingbird Speaking."

Sarah waited for him to tell her more about his mother but he had turned his attention to the basket of water. Using two wet sticks, he took hot stones from the fire and

It was pretty obvious. The hot stones were making the water hot. He was heating water for tea.

When the bread was toasted and the tea was brewed, Charlie thanked Mother Earth, praising her beauty and her bounty, and promising to use her gifts carefully. "*Mitakuye oyasin,*" he said, smiling at Sarah.

"Is that Cahuilla language?" she asked.

"No, it's what the Sioux say in ceremony. It means 'We are related to all things.'"

As they ate, he told her about the Cahuillas who, generations ago, lived on acorns, mesquite beans, pinyon seeds, meat from small animals, greens from along the streams and dates from the fan palms.

"The desert was their health food store. Now we live on pizza. Our elders say it makes us soft. But I love pizza."

"So do I," Sarah said.

"Well, whoever was here last wasn't eating pizza," Charlie said scooping up a handful of tiny bones and handing them to her.

"What are they?"

"Quail."

"Oh, dear."

"It's all right," Charlie said. "They weren't shot for sport and their little bodies gave some other animal life. Passed it along in a sacred circle. If you can find a few wishbones, we should take them along."

"What for?"

"Fishhooks."

Sarah giggled, remembering a girl at school who refused to believe there could be fish in the desert. Of course, the fish in Magic Canyon were too tiny to hook, but in Utah Mama had photographed a fish that weighed four pounds. She told Charlie about the

fish, about Mama and then, before she knew it, she was telling him about her first dream, the awful vision of Mama trapped in the canyon, in danger, in need of help.

"I tried to tell my father this dream but he's a scientist and when I started talking about holes in the sky and poison dripping from clouds, he hit the ceiling. He said I was too old for fairy tales. Is he right?"

"Yes," Charlie said, "if you put it that way. But your father speaks a different language. He uses different words for what you are describing—ozone layer, pollution, erosion, acid rain. In scientific language, your dream might make a lot of sense to him."

"Wow!" Sarah said. "You really do know all about dreams."

"No," Charlie said. "Nobody does and I know less than my elders. I do know that your father is right about one thing: dreams are not fairy dust you can sprinkle on a problem to make it go away. They're more like star charts. They can help us figure out where we are and how we fit into the pattern of the universe. But we have to study them, think about them.

"My spiritual teacher, William Songchanter, told me that in his experience, when a person has a vision, a short time later, he or she usually receives a sign, something tangible in the real world, that repeats or verifies the dream. He says that when you have a vision it is important to be patient. Like the turtle—which many Indian legends say supports the whole world."

Charlie laughed. "I'm a fine one to talk about turtles and patience. I dreamed about a bulldozer and before dawn I was out building a fire on one. Luckily Songchanter and the Badger Society elders were patient with me. They put up my bail but they told me that I needed to think long and hard about what my vision could mean. They said that a true vision is almost always followed by a physical sign—sometimes more than one. So that's what I've been doing up here on the sacred mountain."

"Waiting for a sign?"

"Yes."

"Did you get one?"

"No, I had another vision and I learned something important."

"What?"

"To be a turtle," Charlie said, laughing. "Come on, I'll take you home."

"You think I should go home and wait for a sign?"

"I'm sure of it."

Sarah stared at the embers of their little fire. Soon it would be ashes. They should bury them so that the cave would be familiar and friendly for the animals.

"There was a hummingbird in my dream," Sarah said, sipping the last of her tea. "And a badger. They danced with us." She talked softly, with her eyes closed, telling her dream but seeing it too, so vividly it was as if she was there again—dancing with Mama and the animals, following Badger, watching Indian Rock

come alive, seeing pictures of the places she was supposed to photograph. Every detail was crystal-clear.
The Indian's words. His turtle ring. The hummingbird at her feet when the dream faded.

She stopped talking. The fire was out. Charlie
was staring at her.

"Sarah," he said, "why did the Indian call you
Star?"

"Because it's my middle name, the name my
mother called me. I feel like it's my real name."

Softly, as if he were thinking out loud, Charlie
said, "A chip of brightness, a piece of meteorite, perhaps a star."

"What?"

"In my vision," Charlie said, "I saw a ring of
rocks and boulders, a huge medicine circle. A bulldozer came and began shoving them apart. I kept
trying to push them back into place but they were
too heavy. Then I saw a bright speck on the ground.
I picked it up and held it out and it worked like a
magnet, drawing the boulders to it, moving them
back in place, restoring the sacred circle."

Sarah's eyes widened. "Maybe the star you saw
in your vision is me. Maybe Mother Earth
wants us to go on this journey together. To
save a whole lot of places like Magic Canyon.
Your vision, my dreams. It all fits. Like puzzle
pieces. That's the sign we're both waiting for. It
has to be."

She jumped up, but Charlie stayed where he was,
staring into the fire, thinking. Finally he began to
speak, slowly, in a way that made her know that
the questions he was asking were important. "In
your dream. That Indian. Did you know him?
Was he someone you had seen before?"

"No."

"What did he look like? What was he wearing?"

"He was tall and straight with snow-white hair and he wore a necklace with sharp, curved prongs around it."

"Bear claws."

"Yes."

"And a buffalo robe . . ."

"With birds and stars painted on it."

"Yes."

"And he had a ring on his finger."

"Set with a turtle carved from a red stone."

"Yes, yes, how did you know?" Sarah cried.

"How did *you* know?" Charlie said. "You are describing William Songchanter, his bear claw necklace, his white buffalo robe and the sacred turtle ring he always wears on the first finger of his right hand."

For a moment they sat in stunned silence. Then Sarah jumped up and did a badger dance around the cave. Her jacket flapped like wings and something fell from the pocket. She bent, picked it up and held it out for Charlie to see. A small red stone in the shape of a turtle.

They left the cave the way Charlie had entered, down a long tunnel to a small opening high up on the rock wall. He made his hands into a stepping stone so Sarah could climb out, and they covered the opening with mesquite and creosote branches because the entrance was a Cahuilla secret.

They walked fast and made it to Pine Crest in under four hours. The bus station was deserted but there was a man in a striped shirt at the ticket counter. He was reading the sports page of the newspaper, listening to the radio, eating a sugar doughnut and sipping coffee from a paper cup. "Two tickets for Lupine Springs," Sarah said, in what she hoped was a grown-up voice.

Without looking up, the man issued the tickets, made change and fiddled with the radio dial. Country and western music was replaced by local news.

"A distraught father and an Indian activist are leading search parties in a wild canyon in the California desert looking for a lost child. Last seen around nine o'clock last night, eleven-year-old Sarah Stewart was missing from her bed when her father went to wake her at eight-thirty this morning. The authorities are appealing to the public for information because although the search is centering on the canyon where the child frequently wanders, police have not ruled out the possibility that she is a runaway or the victim of an abductor."

Sarah stifled a gasp, stuffed the tickets and money in her pocket and with her heart pounding, forced herself to walk slowly away from the ticket window and out the door. Charlie was sitting on a bench, his face turned up to the sun. "Here," she said, handing him a bus ticket. "We'd better not sit together. They're looking for me. The police think I'm lost or the victim of an abductor. I heard it on the radio. The announcer said that my father and an Indian activist have been in the canyon together today searching for me. You're the only Indian activist we know, and you're here with me. Who do you think they are talking about?"

"Your guess is as good as mine."

"I think we should hide in the bushes until the bus comes."

"I think you should call your father. He's obviously frantic."

"I know, but it's too dangerous to call from here. I'll call him from Lupine Springs."

"Well," Charlie said, "it's your decision but I think it's cruel of you to torture him with worry. You could at least let him know that you're alive and well."

"Oh, Charlie," Sarah sighed. "You're worse than my conscience. But you're right. Only we'll probably get caught."

"If so, it will be a sign."

But they didn't get caught, although Sarah made the call again and again, in Pine Crest and at bus stops along the way. The line was always busy.

Finally, in Lupine Springs, she got the answering machine which startled her with a new message, recorded in her father's voice: "If it's you, Sarah, please, please tell me where you are and how I can reach you. Anyone with even a clue about what has happened to my little girl, please leave a message and a phone number so I can call you back."

Tears sprang to her eyes. "I'm all right, Daddy," she said. "I'm fine. Really! I'm with Charlie. You can't reach me because we'll be in the wilderness, but we'll be back in a few days. I'll call you then."

Lupine Springs was a medium-size town, a touristy place full of motels, restaurants and gift shops selling souvenirs. The streets were clogged with out-of-state cars and there were a quite a few gas stations and bars. Looking around, Charlie said, "If I were planning a vision quest, this is the last place I'd pick."

"I know, but this is where we start our hike," Sarah said, excitedly.

"After we buy some food."

"Can't we live on edible plants?"

Charlie said that although the ancient Cahuilla did live on desert plants, it took whole villages to do the gathering, sifting, leaching, soaking, grinding and roasting to make things like acorns and agave roots edible. An agave cabbage, for example, had to be baked in fire pit for at least twenty-four hours. Then it was tender and juicy, layered with a sweet, molasses-like syrup—delicious and very nutritious. Raw, it was too tough to chew and swallow, much less digest. Taking a jackrabbit down with a throwing stick was a better idea.

And a trip to the supermarket was the best idea of all. In the market, they shopped carefully. Nothing perishable. No cans because cans are heavy. Walking along the asphalt road that led out of town was hot and boring, but they plodded ahead, doggedly, until Sarah found what she was looking for—a dirt road, veering off to the right and almost immediately branching off in three directions. "We go left, Charlie," she said.

It looked like one of those roads that begin as an animal trail and end up at some dry hole where water had once been. But the road went on and on, twisting and turning, always uphill. Soon they left the sagebrush behind. An old juniper, its gray trunk streaked with red, leaned a scraggly limb across the road. Then there were more junipers, young, healthy ones. Finally, the road filtered like the wind through columns of tall ponderosa pine.

They stopped in the forest, a spacious, airy place, with an arched ceiling of branches overhead and a thick carpet of needles underfoot. All the clues had worked. This was the place. Sarah was ecstatic.

Charlie was asleep. He was sitting up with his back against a tree trunk, a shaft of late afternoon sun falling across his knees, his eyes closed and breathing so silently he might have been a statue. Her father would have forced himself to stay awake to take care of her. Even then, he would have warned her not to wander off, not to get lost.

She liked not being told what to do. With Charlie, it was almost like being on her own. Suddenly, she was immensely happy. They had left behind the world of responsibilities and manners, warnings and questions, the telephone and time. She took her watch off and put it in her backpack. The sun and the stars were all they needed now.

Soon she had something interesting to watch. In a patch of sunlight a few feet away, two tassel-eared squirrels went about their business making it look like play, scampering up and down tree trunks like circus performers, bridging the distance between branches with arching leaps and graceful sweeps of their gray-white tails. Winter was over and the sun was warm on their fur. The time of feasting had come.

The squirrels moved to and from their banquet table which was a particularly luxurious pine. Gleefully, they clipped twig ends and stripped them to get at the juicy flesh within. Carelessly, they strewed the ground with the twigs they had chewed. But they were not littering. They were obeying a law of nature. It was not necessary for them to know it, but Mother Earth would soon send jackrabbits to feed on the clipped twig ends. Recycling was no big deal the way the animals did it. They just played the roles assigned to them in the carefully balanced circle of life.

It was almost dark when Charlie woke up. Sarah expected him to ask what she had been doing. Sometimes her father even asked what she was thinking. Charlie just began slicing bread. Indians, she was beginning to see, didn't litter the air with questions. If she had something she wanted to tell him he would stop what he was doing and give her his complete attention. Otherwise, her thoughts and her actions were her own.

They ate the food they had bought in Lupine Springs. They did not need a fire and it was still light when they finished. Charlie took out his knife and the quail bones they had found in Magic Canyon. Sarah watched him cut and sharpen the bones and notch the hook shanks. He tied each hook to a fishing line, wrapped the joint with silky, yellowish brown fibers and sealed it with a gob of sticky pine pitch from a tree.

"Nature's Band-Aid," Charlie said, dabbing a bit of the pine pitch on a cut on the back of his hand. "It's waterproof, there's plenty of it, it seals just about anything—and you can chew it like gum."

He wrapped the fishhooks in a piece of canvas and put the package into his storage bag.

When he turned around, Sarah's jaws were going up and down. "It tastes like butterscotch," she said. "Sort of."

•6•

When Sarah awoke the next morning, Charlie was sitting on a rock studying a map they had bought in Lupine Springs. "Sarah," he said, "the United States Geological Survey seems to have lost the Lost Falls you saw in your dream."

He did not seem to expect an answer and Sarah did not have one so she folded her groundcloth. Sleeping on pine needles sure beat sleeping on the rock floor of a cave.

"Aha," Charlie said, pointing to the text on the back of the map. "It says here that Lost Falls were mentioned in cavalry reports of the 1890s. They're described as 'wide, blue-green waterfalls on a sharp bend of the Silver Woman River.'"

"We'll find them," Sarah said, eating a piece of bread. Her dream pictures were still clear and she was feeling confident. After all, the clues had led them to this forest which Charlie said was directly above a sharp bend of the Silver Woman River. There was a spring in the forest so they could fill their bottles and canteens and have enough water to last until they found their way down to the river. Everything was working out perfectly.

They set out early and took everything with them because they did not know how long the trek would take. They might have to spend the night and return tomorrow. Return where? Here, perhaps, but not necessarily. They were on a journey and while they were on it, home would be wherever they happened to be. The idea made Sarah feel gloriously free. Before roads and fences and laws and land deeds, the Indians must have felt this way every day of their lives.

A wind blew as they walked along the rim of a canyon that

was identified on the map as Broken Knife Canyon. Sarah looked over the edge and knew she could never put into words what she saw and felt. Terrifying. Dizzying. Majestic. Broken Knife Canyon was a gigantic red slash in the earth. Sheer rock walls fell away to empty air below. In the early morning sun, everything was either blood-red or black shadow. Compared to this, the canyons she knew—Magic, Cactus, Serina—were comfortable and cozy. If Silver Woman River was down there, Sarah couldn't see it, and if seeing it meant leaning out very far, she didn't want to try.

The cavalry report said that there was no usable trail to the river in this area, but Charlie was looking for one. It was quite possible that an Indian trail would have been considered unusable by a cavalryman. After fifteen or twenty minutes, Charlie stopped, bent down, examined something, stood up again and looked over the canyon rim.

"Looks like we've found it," he said. "A trailhead. See that?" He pointed to a limestone boulder. Sarah looked and saw scratches on the rock. Wavy lines, circles, animals with horns. In Magic Canyon there were similar pictures on rocks, painted by Indians hundreds of years ago. They were called pictographs. Pictures cut into the rock were called petroglyphs. She'd learned the difference in school.

"Do you think they were scratched with a knife and the knife broke and that's why it's called Broken Knife Canyon?" she asked.

Charlie didn't answer. He was studying the petroglyphs. Some of the picture writing, he said, was very old. Some of it was more recent. He pointed to a drawing of an animal that looked like an antelope. A line ran from the animal's mouth to its heart. "The Hopi and the Navajo used a line like that to represent the voice of the hunter, reaching the animal, bringing it near. Hunting magic."

He unscrewed the top of Sarah's water bottle and splashed water on the rock. Faint paintings done in red and black showed up. There was a wavy line that Charlie said usually meant water or river, a stick figure and a spiral with a straight line at the bottom—a symbol meaning south or down. He said you could spend a lifetime studying petroglyphs and pictographs. There were so many theories. Were they art, religion, a way of recording history? Probably all three.

"I also think," Charlie said, "that sometimes our ancestors wrote on rocks simply to give directions—to a village, to a good hunting area, to a sacred hill or cave—and, I hope, to Silver Woman River. Shall we try it?"

The trail was steeper than any Sarah had seen or imagined, a series of switchbacks, following ledges, inching down the rock wall. At first her knees were weak with fright. After a while she got used to it. As they zigzagged down, the rocks around them turned from sandy yellow to dark red.

"Hermit shale," Charlie said. "Iron oxides wash out of it onto the rocks below. That's what makes the canyon red." Later he showed her a place where the limestone jutted out into the canyon, away from the overhanging shale. Here the limestone was gray like the boulders in Magic Canyon and the other canyons Sarah knew. She thought about this as she plodded silently, steadily downward in the growing heat. Rocks, and people, could be the same but look different because they had a different color skin. Or because something had happened to them.

They stopped to drink in a shady place where the trail threaded its way between gray rock walls. Sarah sat down but Charlie was examining the rock wall. "Look," he said, pointing.

"What are they?" she asked.

"Bits and pieces of coral, shells, starfish and sea lilies that lived long ago."

"How long ago?"

"250 million years."

"How did they get way up here?"

"In those days, way up here was way down there and way down there was an ocean."

They set out again. Down, down, down. Hotter with each

step. After a while, Sarah said what she was thinking. "When are we going to get there?"

"Why?"

"I feel like I'm burning up and this trail is so steep my toes are hitting the front of my boots and my knees are starting to ache."

She waited for him to say something comforting. Instead he asked, "Is that all?"

"What do you mean?"

"I mean it sounds like you're still in pretty good shape. That's good because the trail is getting steeper and the sun is getting hotter. A couple of hours from now, you may have blisters on your heels, cuts and scratches on your shins, a bruised elbow, a cactus thorn in your finger. Just don't turn an ankle."

A couple of hours? Cuts and bruises? Sarah was horrified. But maybe he was just trying to scare her, trying to get her to give up and turn back. Well, it wouldn't work. She was going on.

She comforted herself with thoughts of the river. Silver Woman. The name had a lovely, sparkling sound. She imagined plunging her arms, elbow-deep in crystal-clear cold water, splashing it on her face, wading in it, soaking her bandanna and tying it wet and cool around her neck.

But it was getting hotter. Heat came down from the sky and up from the trail, bounced off sidewalls, beat about her face like the flapping of fiery wings. She was getting dizzy from the turns in the path. They stopped to eat the sandwiches they had brought but Sarah was too hot and tired to eat more than a bite. She chewed a little trail mix and drank some water. They crouched in a sliver of shade to rest and then went on.

The rest helped a little but Sarah's heart was heavy and grew heavier with each downward step. The closer they moved to Silver Woman River, the more frightened she became. Shouldn't they be hearing it? At this time of year Magic Canyon was full of water sounds, murmurs, gurgles, trickles, swooshes, the thunder of waterfalls. Long before you got to the stream, you could hear it singing its watery song. Now, in Broken Knife

Canyon, every sound in the world seemed to have been drained away by the sun. Even the lizards lay motionless in the dead silence.

She wanted to ask Charlie how far it was to the river and why they couldn't hear it, but she knew it was a foolish question. They'd get there when they got there and if there was no water in the river, they would know it soon enough and it would not be a good thing to know.

It took them half the day to reach the bottom of the canyon and going back up would be harder and take twice as long. Trying to walk along those ridges in the dark would be suicide, but they didn't have enough water to wait for daylight and then climb all day in the heat. Most of all, she was afraid she wouldn't have the strength. She could hardly stagger downhill. Climb back up? She'd never make it. She thought of the movies she'd seen, the stories she'd heard. Covered wagons losing the trail. Men chasing gold. Scratching the sand for water. Dying under the blazing sun.

Her eyes burned, her throat ached, her feet were blistering. Soon she would simply fall down and be unable to get up. What a way to end a vision quest. A pile of bleached bones.

But Charlie was stronger. If he were alone, he might be able to save himself, might somehow manage to climb out of the canyon. She would have to persuade him to leave her. She would give him what was left of her water. No sense wasting water on a person who was about to die. The thought brought tears to her eyes, and one tear ran down her cheek. Stop it, Sarah, she said to herself. The first law of desert survival is don't waste water!

She decided to make her mind a blank, to concentrate her attention on the trail which was a jumble of loose rocks. Ankle-breakers, her father called them. The going was rough but they were almost to the bottom of the canyon.

Sarah thought she was ready for the worst, but she must have been secretly hoping against hope because when they reached the river and found it bone-dry, she was overwhelmed with disappointment. She was also bewildered and angry. Her dream had betrayed her. It had tricked her into leading herself and Charlie Night into a death trap. Poor Charlie. He wouldn't be here except for her. She turned to say something to him but he was no longer beside her. He had moved off about a hundred yards and was walking briskly along the dry riverbed. She followed, hurrying to catch up, not because she wanted to but because there didn't seem to be anything else to do. He went on and on. He was going too fast. She began to stumble. "Charlie," she called in a parched voice. "Stop."

He stopped at once and turned around. She held out her water bottle.

"Take it," she said. "And go back. I can't do this anymore." Then, her anger returning, she said defiantly, "And I don't want to."

He stayed where he was, a few yards away from her. "What about your dream?" he asked.

"My dream was wrong."

"You can't know that until you've given it your best, tried your utmost."

"I've done that. I've reached my limit."

"And you think a vision quest is about limits? That's a camping trip. A vision quest is about going beyond the things that limit us—weakness, pain and fear. It's about doing more than our best. It's not an expedition to explore the desert. It's an expedition to explore the self, the soul, the spirit."

He took the water bottle from her, unscrewed the cap, handed the open bottle to her and told her to drink. When she did, he told her to drink some more. She protested. They would run out of water. Her dream was not to be trusted. It said there would be a waterfall below the sharp bend in Silver Woman River.

"There may be," Charlie said.

"There can't be a waterfall in a river that doesn't have any water in it."

"A logical theory that may or may not be true. We can test it. But what I need to know first is whether you have decided to give up or go on. You have the power to do either one."

Sarah did not think she had the power to take even one step but she determined to take it. At least she would die facing her dream, not turning her back on it.

To her surprise, she had taken quite a few steps when Charlie stopped. "Put your ear to the ground," he said.

Sarah got down on her hands and knees. Her palms burned but she was past caring. She laid her ear against the hot flat rocky riverbed and heard the most beautiful sound in the world, the sound of water. She stood up and stared at Charlie.

"Silver Woman has gone underground," he said. "She may come out somewhere downstream." He turned and continued walking, following the dry stream bed. Sarah followed. She wanted to ask where and when and how far he thought it would be to the place where Silver Woman might or might not come out of hiding. But that would take energy and she needed every ounce of strength to put one foot in front of the other. "Finish what you start," her father always said. She could hear him saying it now and it steadied her waves of dizziness.

The dry riverbed twisted and turned. One more bend, Sarah told herself. Just one more. But there was always another turn ahead. Her ankles and knees ached and her boots skidded this way and that on the rounded stones. The canyon filled with shadows but they were not cool shadows because the rock walls were still hot from baking in the sun all day. She walked like a sleepwalker, not looking around, sure that there was nothing to see, that everything around them was dead.

Suddenly, around a sharp bend, a mass of green and gold lit up the gloom. It looked like a grove of cottonwood trees gleaming in the late afternoon sun. They couldn't be real.

But they were. Before she reached the tall shimmering trees, she could smell their freshness. It revived her. She knew that smell and what it meant. Charlie waited for her to catch up and they walked together to the place where Silver Woman rose out of the sand in a crystal-clear torrent.

They drank, filled the water bottles, plunged their hands and arms into the water and splashed it on their faces. Then, wordlessly, they walked on, following the river.

At dusk, a great horned owl swooped down in front of them. Then, suddenly, there it was. In the fading light, Lost Falls looked like a grand staircase with blue-green water pouring over it. Each stairstep was a quiet pool, as if the river were resting before taking another plunge.

Sarah spread her groundcloth on a mossy bank. "I think I'll take a little sleep before it's time to sleep," she said to Charlie. She thought he smiled but she was unlacing her boots, lying down, feeling the ache drain away and the energy of Mother Earth pulsing beneath her. Moss was the softest bed of all.

When she woke she smelled smoke. Charlie had started a fire and was cleaning four trout he had pulled from the river. He threaded one on a sharpened stick and held it out to her. "Here," he said, "you can help cook our Thanksgiving feast."

Thanks. Giving. For the first time, the name of the holiday was real to her. Every year she had celebrated Thanksgiving Day—with roast turkey and cranberry sauce and pumpkin pie, decorations on the table and stories and songs about the Pilgrims surviving a starvation winter with the help of the Indians. Now Sarah knew what the Pilgrims must have felt. Clean, stripped-down joy. She was alive and life was dear and lovely on a bountiful earth. She had a blister on her right foot and her knee was throbbing, but her heart was singing. She looked around and felt an immense love for everything her gaze fell upon—the moss, the cottonwood trees, the bright little fire, the silvery trout and the blessed, cool, clear water. Such good and perfect gifts. All freely given.

"I'll be right back," she said to Charlie. She ran to the river's edge and without thinking she spread her arms wide and lifted them high. "Thank you, Silver Woman," she sang out. "Thank you Mother Earth and Father Sky."

She hurried back to where Charlie was kneeling beside the fire. "I think," he said, looking up at her, "that you have grown taller today."

Sarah grinned with pleasure. At school, she was often praised but it didn't mean much because it was only for doing her homework and obeying the rules. This was different. Hard. Yesterday she would have said impossible. But she had done it, and now she was different. Taller. In one day. "What day is it, anyway?" she asked.

"April Fall's Day," Charlie said, "of course."

They whooped and hollered with laughter. Then they ate. Broiled trout, a salad of watercress and dandelion greens, sandwiches left over from lunch and handfuls of sun-warmed wild strawberries. Before the fire died down, Sarah spread her groundcloth under a blossoming redbud and fell asleep listening to Silver Woman singing a river song.

She slept a long time. The sun was filtering through the lavender blooms of the redbud when she sat up and reached for her water bottle. It was wonderful to be able to drink as much as she wanted.

Charlie was gone, his blanket rolled and tied tightly to keep scorpions out. He would be back. The sun would rise higher.

She would find what she had been sent to find. She was happy.

Suddenly she was aware of something moving in the reeds along the river. Cautiously she approached the place to watch. It was Charlie crouching down and popping up like a jack-in-the-box. What on earth could he be doing? He bobbed down and up again. It was like a clown dance. She laughed out loud. Charlie stood up.

"What's so funny?"

"You are. What are you doing? Can I help?"

He said he was catching grasshoppers to use for bait. Even as he was telling her, Sarah saw one and caught it with a graceful swoop of her hand. In a few minutes she had caught five. It was fun finding them, guessing which way they would jump. She didn't even have to crouch down. Sometimes it was an advantage to be small.

She got a bite almost right away. But an olive-green fish with a silvery white belly stole the bait. It happened again and again. That green-and-white fish was a thief!

"No," Charlie said, "he has a right. He was here first."

The green and white fish, Charlie explained, was a humpback chub and native to the area. He and his kind had probably been here since the time of the ancients, long before rainbow trout had been introduced to bring tourists to the area. She should be honored, he said, to be visited by such a rare fish. Because dams had changed their habitat and the foreign fish preyed on them, native fish like the squawfish and humpback were almost extinct. If she caught one, she must carefully unhook it and put it back.

She promised to do so but she wasn't catching any fish and Charlie had caught two big trout. She decided to try her luck downstream. She found a little whirlpool and threw her line in. Almost immediately she felt a nibble, then a bite. She yanked the line hard and it came up empty. "I lost it, I lost it!" she cried.

"The fish?" Charlie asked.

"No, the hook." She was horrified. The little bone hook Charlie had made so carefully was gone.

"No problem," Charlie said, taking her line and handing her his with the remaining wishbone hook tied to it.

"What will you do?" she asked.

"I guess I'll have to let you do the fishing until I make some new hooks."

"With what?"

"The fish bones from last night's supper. In the wilderness, there's no such thing as garbage. Everything is good for something."

They caught three large trout and three small ones. "That's more than we need for one meal, but I think we should smoke some for our journey." He took out his drill stick and hearth board.

"I have matches," Sarah said.

He told her to put them away. In the wilderness, it was important to be able to make a fire without matches. Besides, he was sure she could use the practice on the hearth board.

She knew he was right. Turning the drill by hand was extremely difficult. The aborigines always did it that way but few civilized people were able to manage it. He said she could use a bow. He showed her again how to twist the bowcord once around the drill stick, place the tip of the drillstick in the fireboard socket, move the bow back and forth in a sawing motion, using steady, even strokes until the drill tip was smoking. The trick, her mother had told her, was to gradually spin the drill faster and faster, applying more and more pressure, until there were lots of smoke and black dust.

"But before you even begin," he said, "make sure you have a bundle of really good tinder. Of course what you use will depend on where you are. Around here, we can shred the dead leaves around the base of yucca plants, get fibers from the dried stalks of the milkweed and silk fibers from the pods. We can also use cliffrose bark and the inner layer of bark on some of those dead cottonwood trees. It's worth hunting for good tinder because the spark will be very tiny, very brief."

She was slow, uncoordinated, clumsy, failed again and again,

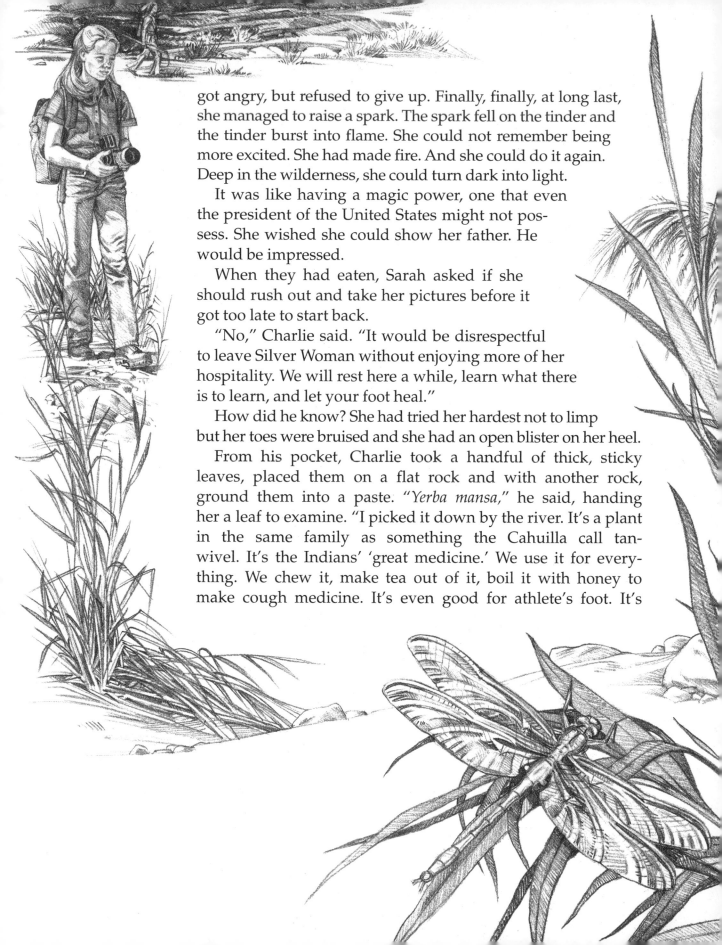

got angry, but refused to give up. Finally, finally, at long last, she managed to raise a spark. The spark fell on the tinder and the tinder burst into flame. She could not remember being more excited. She had made fire. And she could do it again. Deep in the wilderness, she could turn dark into light.

It was like having a magic power, one that even the president of the United States might not possess. She wished she could show her father. He would be impressed.

When they had eaten, Sarah asked if she should rush out and take her pictures before it got too late to start back.

"No," Charlie said. "It would be disrespectful to leave Silver Woman without enjoying more of her hospitality. We will rest here a while, learn what there is to learn, and let your foot heal."

How did he know? She had tried her hardest not to limp but her toes were bruised and she had an open blister on her heel.

From his pocket, Charlie took a handful of thick, sticky leaves, placed them on a flat rock and with another rock, ground them into a paste. "*Yerba mansa*," he said, handing her a leaf to examine. "I picked it down by the river. It's a plant in the same family as something the Cahuilla call tan-wivel. It's the Indians' 'great medicine.' We use it for everything. We chew it, make tea out of it, boil it with honey to make cough medicine. It's even good for athlete's foot. It's

antibacterial as well as soothing. Hold out your foot."

She did. Charlie put the ground leaf paste on the blister and covered it with a whole leaf. Sarah eased her sock on carefully and sat still, watching the canyon world come alive. Goldfinches and buntings and one bright red tanager flitted from cottonwood to mesquite and back. Long-tailed chats shouted and sang and a ladder-backed woodpecker pounded for his dinner.

And there were flowers everywhere. Red, orange, yellow, violet. Monkeyflower, mallow, paperflower, blazing star. She had color film in

her camera and she was in a photographer's paradise.

But when she began thinking about the photographs she was meant to take, all she could think of was the Lost Falls. What was special about them? They were at the bottom of a killer canyon. They had saved her life. But a picture couldn't show that. In a picture Lost Falls would look very much like the waterfalls she had already photographed in Magic Canyon. She went down to the river and pointed her camera at the falls. She tried this angle and that. But nothing looked right. Idly, she pointed the camera straight down at the quiet pool beneath the bank. The water was clearer than the clearest glass. Her finger brushed the shutter and it clicked. The humpback chub swam away.

Later she walked with Charlie downstream to hunt for food and take more pictures. Charlie carried his bow and a handful of arrows with shafts of desert willow and tips of mesquite hardened by fire. He also carried a boomerang-shaped stick made from the branch of a ribbonwood tree. A throwing stick, he called it.

"Looks like this canyon has a lot more jackrabbits than it needs," he said.

"I haven't seen one," Sarah said.

"Neither have I but their tracks and scat are everywhere. Let's go."

"Which way?"

"Wherever you need to go to get your pictures."

So they set off, Sarah trotting ahead like a dog tracking something. Or someone. But she no longer worried that she was the creature being tracked. In this terrifyingly steep-walled red crack in the earth, she was free.

Her tiredness had gone, her blisters no longer hurt. The canyon widened and a sandy beach appeared

along the river. The sand was cool and soft underfoot so that she fairly danced along. Faster and faster she skipped, leaving Charlie behind.

Rounding a curve, she caught her breath and stopped. In front of her the river narrowed and on the sandy bank was a deer. Only it wasn't a deer. It was a delicate little pronghorn, only four feet high, honey-beige with patches

of white on its rump, flanks, throat and cheeks. A female, but wearing horns, as both male and female pronghorns do, holding its head high. Proudly, Sarah thought.

Moving more silently than she dreamed she could, Sarah got the lens cap off her camera and took a photograph. The pronghorn did not move. It was the most beautiful creature in the world and in a minute Charlie might shoot it. "Go! Go!" she cried, clapping her hands.
"Run away. Run away!"

Charlie was beside her but the little antelope had disappeared into the bristly graythorn thicket that bordered the sand. It was safe. Pronghorns, her mother said, could run forty-five miles an hour.

"I scared away our dinner," she said to Charlie. "I'm sorry but I couldn't bear to let you shoot it. If we find anything else, you can have my share."

Charlie said nothing.

"Are you angry?"

"No, no, little star," he said, more gently than she had heard him speak before. "It is good to have a kind heart and to make unselfish choices."

They walked on. The path was level and shady. Leading the way, Sarah came to a huge tangle of wild grapevines. "Look, Charlie," she said, cupping a bunch of green grapes in her hand. "They're almost ripe."

"Yes," he said, bending down, "but look at this." On the ground, hidden under the vines, was a nest. In it were twelve quail eggs.

"Are you going to take them?"

"No. They're too small to provide very much nourishment. They represent new life, and we're not starving. We can eat the fish we smoked if we don't find something else."

As if to fulfill his prophecy, on the way back to camp, they came upon green and yellow squash growing on a flat patch of land where the canyon widened and the river slowed. A long time ago someone had farmed here. A hundred years ago? A thousand? Only Silver Woman knew.

· 8 ·

One by one the burning twigs that had been their cooking fire turned from red to black to gray. One by one the stars came out.

"Now," Charlie said, "about those questions you've been storing up all day."

There were a million questions Sarah had been wanting to ask but now she had forgotten them or they had answered themselves or they didn't seem important anymore. But there was one thing she still wanted to know. "How did you know that Silver Woman River was flowing underground?"

"Because I'm a geologist. Remember?"

She remembered the reporter telling her that but she found it hard to believe. A geologist was a scientist, a person like her father, someone who didn't believe in vision quests or spirit-calling ceremonies. "But you're a Cahuilla Indian," she said.

"And you think a person can't be both? A scientist and an Indian?"

"Well, sort of," she said, hoping she hadn't said anything wrong.

"Once I thought that, too," Charlie said. "But the more science I study the more respect I have for the ancient beliefs my people revere and celebrate. It's not necessary to choose. I believe both."

For a while Sarah sat quietly, thinking about what he was saying. She and Mama had talked like this. "My mother said that what we call truths are openings in the mind to let the light of the Creator shine through. The openings are different sizes and shapes but the light is the same and it is brighter than anything we can imagine."

"She was right. Before books or television or schools, the ancients knew, understood and lived a great truth that science is rediscovering: *Mitakuye oyasin*. We are all related. Connected. Inseparable. People talk about getting back to nature. But we can't leave nature. Whatever we do, good or bad, affects the rest of the natural world and everything that happens in the natural world affects us. It's an old idea but it seemed new to me. I began to look at my life, my work, the landscape, with different eyes. I saw that many of the things environmentalists are now discovering, the Indians have known for centuries. Suddenly I wanted to know more. So I began studying with an ancient holy man, William Songchanter. But there is so much to learn, it seems as if it will take a lifetime," Charlie laughed. "When I said that to Songchanter he said that learning is what a lifetime is for."

It was a long story, but in the canyon there seemed to be all the time in the world. The fire went out. A small wind that had ruffled the grass at dusk, crept away. Still they sat in silence but, it seemed to Sarah, not alone. All the people she and Charlie had been talking about seemed to be there: Mama, Charlie's grandmother and his mother gathering herbs, Charlie as a boy in school, longing to be out under the desert sky, his uncles and aunts performing ritual dances and singing songs about Mukat, the Creator, and all the while, in those long-ago days and now Ursa Major and Ursa Minor, the great starry bears, were prowling the sky, keeping secrets, keeping watch.

The next morning when Sarah woke, the sun was already warm and Charlie had gone off looking for food. He came back with raspberries and duck eggs. They breakfasted and set off to take photographs, walking back the way they had come, following Silver Woman upstream to an animal trail that led away from the river bed and up a steep slope. A plateau lay beyond, a fierce land. Here everything was razor-edged, dagger-shaped, armed with spines. There was no shade and the ground under-

foot was unstable. Sarah skidded on a loose rock and skinned an elbow. Suddenly, they heard thunder. But it wasn't thunder, Charlie said, it was a rockslide somewhere in the distance. Half an hour later they came upon the slide. From somewhere a thousand or more feet overhead, a gigantic boulder had broken off and slid, bounced, gouged and torn its way down the canyon wall. It had landed squarely on the trail, blocking it completely. "Hey," Sarah said, her voice unsteady, "that thing's the size of a garage. What if we had been standing here when it fell?"

But Charlie was looking to the right of the boulder, at a hollowed-out place in the cliff, a small cave or alcove that had been walled up with rocks, most of which the slide had ripped away. "Look," Charlie said.

Using her hand to shield her eyes from the sun, Sarah peered into the little cave. "What is it?"

Carefully, Charlie reached in and brought out something he said was so important that they must put it back where they found it and be careful not to tell everybody and his brother about it because if they did, everybody and his brother would be in here ripping the place up with shovels and backhoes.

Such a little thing, Sarah thought, holding it gently on the palm of her hand. Not a ruin. Not a rock painting. Not a pottery jar. Not even a basket. "What is it?"

"Well," Charlie said, "as you can see it's a tiny animal made of willow twigs. Over the years, quite a few of them have been found in the Southwest. The first one was discovered near a side canyon in the North Rim of the Grand Canyon in the 1930s. Archaeologists think they were made by desert people who lived thousands of years ago."

"It doesn't look very old."

"That's because it's been sealed up in this totally dry place."

"It's so cute," Sarah murmured, wondering if the tiny animal represented a deer or an antelope or a bighorn sheep. Maybe a child had made it. "Was it a toy?"

"Perhaps," Charlie said. "But it may have been made by a hunter and offered to Mother Earth, along with prayers, to thank her for a successful hunting trip in the past or in the future."

"In the future?"

"Yes. Indians give thanks for gifts to come."

"How do they know they will get gifts in the future?"

"Because they believe in the continual goodness of Mother Earth."

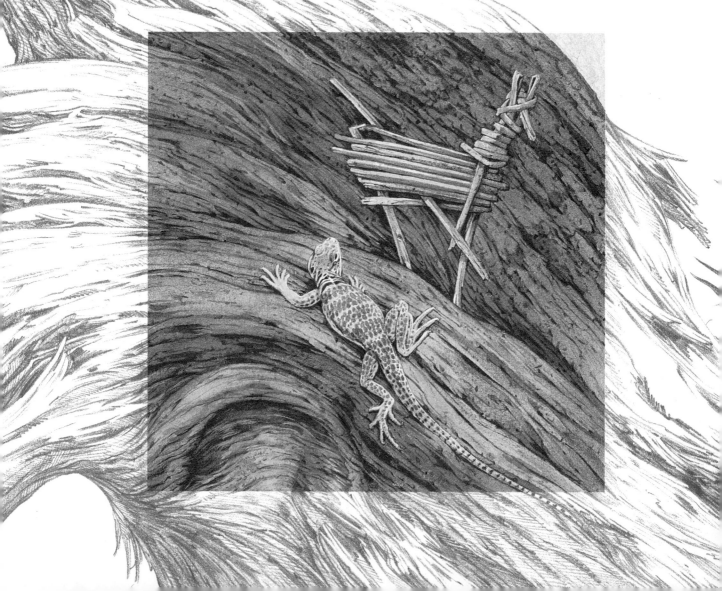

Sarah turned the little stick animal over and saw that its left side was pierced with a splinter of wood. It looked like a spear but she chose to believe it was the hunter's voice reaching the animal's heart.

She posed the twig animal on a cottonwood tree stump and took its picture. Then she dug into her backpack for pencil and paper and made a little sketch. When she finished she put the stick figure back in its little cave and walled it in with stones.

They walked back the way they had come, heading for a rock overhang they had passed on the way. It would shade them while they had lunch. Wherever they went, Charlie carried his full backpack and expected Sarah to carry hers also. Once she had objected, saying that they were going only a short distance, that it wasn't going to get cold, that they couldn't possibly need

[102]

all that water.
Charlie frowned,
picked up her
backpack and
handed it to her.
"Carry it," he said,
and turned away. It
was the first time he had
frowned at her, the first time he
had given her a direct order. She was
furious. How dare he treat her like a child?

She thought about how it was when she went
hiking with her father. Almost always he carried everything in his backpack, enough food and water for them
both. Sarah was free to scamper about like a child. Saying
it to herself, she almost laughed aloud. It was her father
who had treated her like a child. Charlie was treating her
like a person who was old enough to be self-reliant.

After that, Sarah carried her backpack with her wherever she went. Now she leaned against it as she ate, grateful for the rest. She wondered if Charlie ever got tired. If he
did, he didn't show it. He was off now chasing a couple of
jackrabbits they'd seen on the way. She was glad he'd suggested that she wait in the shade.

With half-closed eyes, she watched heat waves shimmer
over a landscape so rocky it might have been the surface of
the moon. A yucca plant growing from a bit of sand
between two boulders held her attention. How beautifully
designed and crafted it was. From a base of dagger-sharp
leaves, three stalks rose tall and straight, each topped with a
cluster of creamy blossoms. An insect droned in the sun. In
the enormous silence of noon, the whole earth was softly
humming. Sarah closed her eyes against the white light and
hummed a little song of her own.

A sound startled her, a small sound, the rattle of stones or pebbles. She left her shady retreat to investigate. On a ledge directly above her stood a magnificent bighorn sheep.

"Hi," she called, expecting the beast to clamber away. The bighorn did not move a muscle. It stood there posing as if for a picture. Sarah went for her camera. When she returned the bighorn was still there. She climbed toward him. With a quick little motion, he leaped to a higher ledge. Sarah followed. Again and again they played that game, Sarah growing more and more determined. "Hold on, Mr. Bighorn," she called after him. "You know you want your picture taken." The sheep was climbing above her, heading over the next rock cropping. This could go on all day, Sarah thought. She reached for her tele-photo lens but before she could sight it, the animal had disap-peared. Higher and higher they climbed, finally reaching a bowl-like plateau. "Got you, Bighorn," she sighed, catching her breath and looking around.

What a lonely, desolate place this was, more remote and hid-den than Broken Knife Canyon itself. Perhaps she was the first

human being in all eternity to set foot here. It was an awesome thought, but even as she was thinking it, something caught her eye.

Less than twenty feet below her, among the rocks and boulders, was a shape that did not make sense. She tried to tell herself that she was looking at a fallen yucca stalk or an odd-shaped rock, but even before she reached it, she knew what she would find.

•9•

Sarah stared at it. What would bring a shovel to a place like this? Even as she asked the question, she thought of an answer. Something men would die to get and kill to keep. Gold.

Nervously she looked around. She had no idea how long the shovel had been here. Its owner might appear at any moment or she might be treading on his bleached bones. No, she told herself, that was silly. Unlike animals, people died with clothes on and there was nothing in sight except the shovel to indicate that a human being had been here. The owner must have left the shovel and gone elsewhere. When and where, to live or die, Sarah had no wish to find out. Not now. Not here. Not alone.

Like a wild creature she heard the age-old voice of instinct telling her to be wary of man. Her first impulse was to break and run, but she resisted. She was not a pronghorn or a mountain goat, and it would be foolish to risk breaking an ankle. She stepped around the shovel and slipped off her pack to put away the camera. She fixed her eyes on an eagle-shaped rock she had passed so that she wouldn't lose her way. Suddenly, the ground under her feet gave out and she plunged straight down into the depths of the earth. She hit bottom with a thud. Gravel, stones, sand and pieces of wood rained down on her head.

She was too startled to cry out and it was some minutes before she was aware of anything except numbing terror. Not daring to move, she sat with her eyes tightly shut, listening. At first she was relieved to hear nothing. Then the silence began to frighten her. She opened her eyes and tried to look around but from blinding brightness she had fallen into total blackness.

She must have fallen into a deep pit. Luckily, something had

broken her fall. She felt around. A heap of canvas. A tent? Whatever it was, it crumbled and fell apart when she touched it. Obviously it had been here a long, long time. Was there a body down here, too? A skeleton? She shuddered and longed for the flashlight in the backpack she had left above. At the same time, she was afraid that more light would show her only that there was no way to get out.

She ached all over and she had skinned her left elbow but everything else seemed to work. She got to her feet and felt around her with outstretched arms. She did not have to reach far in any direction before she hit an absolutely straight-sided wall. Never in a thousand years would she be able to climb out.

"Help!" she screamed, overwhelmed with fear. "Help, help, help, help!" She shouted and shouted in a frenzy of terror but who was there to hear? Charlie had gone off in a downhill direction from their lunch spot. When he returned and found her gone, he would probably expect her to be nearby. He would sit and wait. When he finally did start to look for her, he would have no idea where to look. She had left no clues and in rocky terrain like this, there would be no footprints. Still, she screamed his name until she was exhausted and fell in a heap, sobbing.

Now there were new terrors. Something slithered across her hand, something landed on her cheek. The whole pit was probably full of tarantulas and rattlesnakes. She began clawing at the walls. Dirt and stones rained down on her head, frightening her even more. She must be in a deserted mine shaft. Not good! Mines caved in and buried people alive. She froze, afraid to move a finger.

Slowly, her eyes adjusted, and what had been total blackness became darkness faintly illuminated by a square of daylight high above. Staring at it, she saw that the opening she had fallen through had a board or a beam across it. Willing her heart to stop pounding, she tried to think. Mine shafts were not just holes in the ground. They had to be constructed, with heavy timbers to keep the sides from collapsing inward. She had seen a drawing in the encyclopedia. Carefully she explored the surface of a sidewall with her fingers, looking for beam ends, pegs, ledges—anything she could use for footholds and handholds. No such luck. The wall felt smooth and appeared to rise straight up. Without light, she couldn't even tell whether she was touching wood or stone or packed dirt. How did a blind person ever learn to read braille? Again and again, she went over the same area. Finally she began to detect differences that her fingers transmitted to her brain and her brain turned into pictures. Eventually, she became convinced that the mine shaft was shored up with horizontal boards at three- or four-foot intervals. The boards did not protrude because the earth had moved to fill in the space between them, presenting a smooth surface. It might be possible to dig footholds and handholds in the earthen strips between the boards. She could probably find a sharp stone to dig with but how could she dig and climb with nothing to hang on to? Halfway up, she would fall backward and break her neck.

She thought of the rock climbers who came from all over to climb a famous cliff face back home. It was called the Wall, and she used to go there with her father to watch. The climbers used ropes and special equipment but her father said that even then, they needed a lot of strength. She didn't have ropes or equipment or any strength at all. It was hopeless she told herself, collapsing on the heap of canvas and starting to sob.

Suddenly, she heard Charlie's voice: "A vision quest is not about limits. It is about going beyond the things that limit us—weakness, pain and fear." She reached out to touch him but, of course, he was not there. Still, she was a little ashamed of the way she was behaving. Mama, too, would expect her not only to be good but also to be brave.

She swallowed hard, got up, groped her way to another wall and began to run her hands over it. It might as well have been the same wall, it was so similar. The third and fourth walls were equally disappointing, much too vertical to climb without equipment. At the very least she'd need a rope. Before finishing the thought, she was yanking at the heavy canvas, trying to unfold it. In the olden days, she reasoned, tents were tied down with rope.

She found four pieces of rope, in good condition but somewhat short. Okay, she could tie them together. And then what? Sarah sighed. How was she going to get the rope up to the crossbeam and tie it on?

Well, first things first, she told herself, sitting down with the rope. Right over left and left over right, she chanted, as her father had taught her to do in order to be sure she was making a square knot that would hold instead of a granny knot that might pull apart. Her father, who was a good sailor, knew many knots and had taught her a few of the most useful ones.

Tying square knots was satisfying but trying to throw a rope fifteen feet up and over a crossbeam was frustrating. Again and again it fell short. It needed something heavy on the end to carry it over. A stone. Plenty of stones around, but attaching one to the end of a thick rope was harder than it looked. In fact, it turned out to be impossible. If there was a knot that would do it, Sarah didn't know it and couldn't figure it out.

And her left ankle hurt. She unlaced her boot and took it off, dislodging a small stone that had been pressing against her ankle bone. For a long time she sat quietly with her boot off, almost able to see in the darkness now that her eyes had become used to it. The wall to climb would be the one to her left. It leaned outward ever so slightly, especially at the top where a portion of earth had actually fallen away in a minor landslide. Probably caused by me, she thought, slipping her foot into her boot and beginning to do up the laces. Suddenly she stopped, took off the boot and stared at it.

"Why not?" she said aloud. Setting the boot down, she

picked up the rope and tied what her father said might be the most useful knot in the world, the bowline. Then she picked up her boot and threaded both laces, in opposite directions, through the loop formed by the bowline knot. Using her dear old square knot, she tied the laces together and regarded her handiwork: a rope weighted at one end with something almost as heavy as a stone. It just might work.

It took more than a dozen throws but finally Sarah managed to get the boot to carry the rope over the crossbeam and back down to where she could reach it. Carefully, she untied the boot, threaded the free end of the rope through the bowline loop and pulled. Obediently the loop traveled up to the crossbeam tightening the rope around it. She had aimed her throws so that now, as she had hoped, the rope hung close to the left-hand wall where she could use it to steady and hoist herself as she dug footholds and handholds and climbed. She put on her boots, found a sharp stone and began to dig. After that it was all aching and straining, muscles burning and knees quivering with exhaustion, slipping and sliding, stabs of terror and lunges for the rope. She could not spare the effort for a single thought, not for hope or despair or for what would happen if she did or did not get out.

Even when she at last hauled herself over the crumbling edge of the pit and crawled to safe ground, she lay for a long time in a kind of daze, registering only that the desperate effort was over. Her throat burned, her lips were cracked, but all she could do was gasp for air and shut her eyes against the sun.

She had no idea how long she lay there but when she opened her eyes, Charlie was kneeling beside her with a water bottle. She tried to tell him what had happened, tried to thank him for coming to find her, but she was too tired, too thirsty.

When they got back to camp, Sarah sat beside the river while Charlie made supper. She took her boots off and dangled her feet in the cool, clear water. What an incredible thing it was

to be alive, even if you were scratched and bruised and bone-tired. The earth was so beautiful—the river, the rustling cotton-wood leaves, the faint hoot of a distant owl, the fragrant air, the luminous sky.

Tonight, Charlie said, there would be a full moon. It would light their way so that they could climb out of the canyon in the cool of night.

Sarah was astonished at the beauty of Broken Knife Canyon by moonlight. How frightening it had seemed on the way down. Empty and dead. Now it was full of memories and friends. She hated to leave. In the shadows all around her, just out of sight, she sensed the presence of eyes, paws, hooves, wings—wild things that had shared their home with her and had asked nothing in return. It was not often that way in the world they were going back to.

Just before dawn, they reached a rock platform at the foot of the talus slope leading up to the steepest cliffs. They stopped there to rest and greet the new day. Charlie burned a few sprigs of juniper and as the fragrant smoke rose, he spoke to the four points. North, the main power that holds the others in place. South, where the first badger ran to get fire and bring it back to earth. West, the jagged edge of the world, the place of mystery and dreams. Charlie thanked each direction for its gifts and then he faced east, the place of beginning, and sang to the new sun. Aiee, aiee, aiee. Fierce and free, the sound swooped and soared like a wild eagle in the endless air. Sarah's scalp tingled with something like fear. But it was recognition. She realized, for the first time, that human beings were wild things, too. In places like Broken Knife Canyon, they found a part of them-selves they did not know they had lost.

It took hours to climb the rest of the way and Sarah was exhausted when they reached the spring under the Ponderosa pines. Two squirrels crept as close as they dared and looked on with curious eyes. Sarah was sure they were the same squirrels

she had observed before. One had a notch out of its left ear and the other had a curious way of lifting its right front paw.

She wondered if they recognized her. She had been gone only a few days but she had changed—in ways that people might not notice but an animal might sense. She had been angry and sad and worried and in such a frantic rush that she couldn't think or feel. Now she knew that saving the earth was not something you did, it was a way of being. It was the way you saw animals and trees and rocks, the way you felt about them.

And it was not something solemn and grim. What the squirrels were doing was important but they did it joyfully. Worry had no place in Mother Earth's beautiful design. Somehow the awesome wildness of Broken Knife Canyon had taught her that.

What they had to do now, Charlie said, was to rest. Sitting up with his back against a tree trunk, he closed his eyes and immediately fell asleep. Sarah still wasn't able to do that. She decided to see how still she could sit. She sat so still that one of the squirrels grew bold enough to investigate her camera which lay a few inches from her left hand.

Somehow the little creature managed to press the shutter. The click startled him and he ran away along with his companion whose picture he had probably taken.

When Charlie woke up, Sarah told him she had been giving a squirrel photography lessons. "You'll see," she said. "When I get this film developed, there's going to be a picture of a squirrel taken by a squirrel."

They were hungry now but when they got to the highway there was sure to be a convenience store or a gas station that sold food. So they filled their water bottles from the spring and set off. As they walked, Sarah asked how Charlie had managed to find her when she had fallen into the mine shaft. "I was afraid you wouldn't be able to find me because I didn't leave any footprints."

Charlie said that he had learned to track animals in country exactly like Broken Knife Canyon and tracking people was like tracking animals. Only it was easier. He said that people push through vegetation, kick away stones and step on twigs and cactus needles instead of flowing around them the way animals do. Besides, he had a

lot of the information a tracker needs but doesn't always have.

"I knew you were wearing boots. I knew what you were doing as soon as I saw that your camera was gone. And after I tracked you to the first ledge, I knew which direction you were going."

"How?"

Charlie reached into his pocket and handed her three bristly white hairs. "Wild animals move away from people. To a bighorn sheep, away is up."

As they retraced their steps, first along the dirt road, then along asphalt, Sarah thought about the pictures she had taken. Photographing in Magic Canyon had been easy. The animals were old friends—the desert tortoise, the kit foxes, Badger, even the little mare that ran with a herd of wild paints and was so shy that some people did

not believe she was real and said that the canyon was haunted
by a ghost horse.

In Broken Knife Canyon she had taken five pictures, but she
wasn't at all sure what she had managed to get on film. So
much had been going on. So many adventures. A lot of the time
she had been too busy to get her camera out, much less use it.
But with or without pictures, she would remember the pronghorn, the humpback chub, the bighorn, forever.

Now, according to her dream, they were approaching their
final destination: a ghost city hollowed out of a sandstone cliff.
Not a city, exactly, but a village where several families might
have lived. Old, older than the Navajo, older than the Hopi.
Hard to find and hard to climb to, built by ancient people called
the Anasazi. This was a place Sarah's mother had visited when
she was about eighteen. It was one of Sarah's favorite stories. She
liked thinking of her mother as a young girl and the idea of a lost
city enchanted her. "Tell me everything," she used to demand.

"I don't remember everything, honey," her mother had said.
"I know we counted the rooms. There were five, with lots of
balconies and porches and a round room called a kiva for ceremonies and dances."

Now Sarah was telling Charlie the story. How her mother
and a group of friends had been riding horses in the rugged
country near Mesa Verde National Park. From a high cliff they
had seen a mesa that, instead of being green on top, was bright
blue. They decided the color was an illusion caused by the late
afternoon light. But before they turned away, they saw something that interested them more. The blue mesa appeared to
have a ruined cliff dwelling in a cavelike overhang a third of
the way from the top. Darkness was falling, so the young people camped where they were and set off early the next morning
to explore the mesa across the way.

It took all day, but they found the ruin, fallen in and filled
with rubble, but still recognizable as a place where ancient

people once lived. The young people had to be back home by Sunday night so there was time for only a brief look around before they had to leave.

"We said we'd go back," Sarah's mother had told her. "But we never did. Perhaps, one day, you and I will go there together."

"It should be easy to find," Sarah said to Charlie. "A ruin with five rooms and a kiva. After all, how many Anasazi ruins are there around here?"

"Only about a thousand," Charlie said with a smile.

Sarah was shocked. "Really? What if I can't find it? Will you be mad?"

"Of course not," Charlie said. "I volunteered to make this trip and I'm enjoying it. I needed it, too. A drink of wilderness is sometimes as necessary as a drink of water."

Sarah closed her eyes and tried hard to remember every detail of her dream and of her mother's story. "Is there a town called Cortez?"

"Yes, it's near Mesa Verde Park. Is that where you're trying to go?"

"Well, Mama said that the old Indian trail she followed started from Lopez Ranch which is near Cortez. Do you think we can get a bus to Cortez? Do you think Lopez Ranch is still there? Do you think we can find it?"

"I'm beginning to think you can do anything you want to do," Charlie said, chuckling. "Do you think you can find me some chocolate chip ice cream?"

A few minutes later, to Sarah's surprise, she was able to do just that. Although she only half remembered the huge stucco building, with hitching posts out front, they were passing it now. A sign out front said: "The Old Corral. We sell everything in the world."

They entered through swinging doors and found themselves in a maze of aisles and counters and displays. There were shelves of magazines, gifts and souvenirs, charcoal and propane, a camera department, a cosmetic counter, a Western clothing boutique—and an old-fashioned ice cream parlor with twenty-one flavors of ice cream.

They sat on wire chairs in the cool dark of the thick-walled building, eating chocolate chip ice cream served in glass dishes that looked like flowers. After the spare, bright clarity of the desert, this cluttered, shadowy place seemed unreal. But Charlie had already turned his attention to the real world. He had the United States Geological Survey map spread out on the table and was studying it intently. Sarah checked her film supply. "I'll be right back, Charlie," she said. "I'm just going to the camera department for film."

"I'll meet you in the bookstore," he said. "There's a big map of Indian ruins on the wall there that I want to look at."

In the camera department, a television was on but there was no clerk in sight. As she was leaving to find someone to wait on her, Sarah glanced at the television screen and saw something astonishing: her own living room.

Her father was sitting in his armchair and Charlie Night and Corey Blake were sitting on the couch. Corey was speaking. He said that Mr. Stewart and Mr. Night, after working together virtually around the clock for four days, were convinced that the missing child was not in Magic Canyon. It was likely, however, that she was in an even more dangerous situation, lost, perhaps, in a wilderness area with which she was totally unfamiliar.

"Before she disappeared," Corey said, "Sarah talked about making a journey to save endangered canyon areas that are held sacred by Native Americans. There are, of course, hundreds of such places in the Southwest. But Sarah described some of them to her father. Working with these clues, Charlie Night has created a map indicating areas where Sarah might be. Our hope is that showing this map on television will alert people in the vicinity to look for Sarah and call the police or the special hot line. We're trying to keep the home phone free in case Sarah herself calls in."

A map appeared on the screen but Sarah's head was reeling. She must be dreaming. She shut her eyes tight, counted to ten, and then opened her eyes again. The television camera was now focused on Charlie, who seemed to be answering a reporter's question.

"Mr. Stewart told me he needed help from someone who knew Magic Canyon well. We went into the canyon together right away. We've gone out together every day, for four days now—with the police, with the park rangers, the Boy Scouts. Everyone has been trying to help. Yesterday we had almost fifty people searching. But we're not turning up anything new so we're convinced we have to look elsewhere."

"What?" Sarah cried, incredulously. How could Charlie have been searching Magic Canyon with her father when he was catching fish in Silver Woman River, hundreds of miles away? How could he be in her living room in California when he was eating chocolate chip ice cream in Arizona? She turned and ran toward the ice cream parlor. No, Charlie had said he'd meet her in the bookstore. She turned and ran up and down aisles until she located the bookstore. There he was, with his back to her, studying a large, framed map on the bookshop wall.

"Charlie," she shouted from the doorway, "come quick. There's something you've got to see."

She ran quickly up to him and tapped him on the shoulder.

•10•

The figure fell stiffly forward into some rotating racks of paper-backs and maps, and then landed on a floor display of boots.

"Oh, my gosh!" cried Sarah.

Books fell off the racks every which way and skittered across the store floor.

"Hey, kid," the man behind the cash register called. "What's going on?"

"Sorry, oh, I'm really sorry," Sarah stammered as she bent down to lift up the full-sized stuffed Indian figure. "I thought it was my friend. He's tall, with black hair wearing moccasins and a hide shirt, with fringe, and an eagle feather...just like...". She looked at the Indian mannequin. From the front he didn't look anything like Charlie.

"I sure haven't seen anybody like that." He paused, studying her. "But you look familiar. Have we met?"

"No."

"Are you famous or something?"

"No. No. I'm sorry. I have to go. My friend's waiting for me. He's probably outside."

Trying to look calm, she hurried out the front door. Charlie was nowhere in sight. She waited nervously, wishing Charlie would hurry up, afraid to go back into the store to look for him. Any minute now that cashier would figure out why she looked familiar.

The sun was high and hot now and there wasn't a speck of

[126]

shade in front of the building, but along one side, a covered walkway with a deep overhang created a shady strip. Perhaps Charlie was waiting for her there. She went to look. No Charlie. Just two cars and a pickup truck huddled under the overhang like animals trying to stay cool.

She was tempted to do the same, but she was afraid to miss Charlie so she headed for the front door again. As she was rounding the corner of the building she saw something that made her duck back, heart pounding in alarm. A police car was pulling up to the Old Corral. She tried to keep calm. They'd search the building, find Charlie and then come looking for her outside. There was no time to lose and no place to hide.

A dusty brown tarpaulin was folded neatly in the back of the pickup truck which was dark green with a National Park emblem on the side. It wouldn't work but she had to try. She climbed into the truck and pulled the tarpaulin over her. A few minutes later the driver, a park ranger in uniform, returned. He stood in the shade, leaning his back against the truck, so close Sarah was afraid he could hear her breathing. Slowly he unwrapped a candy bar, ate it and put the wrapper in his pocket. Then he hopped into the driver's seat and drove off.

Clutching a corner of the tarp to keep it from flapping, Sarah listened for sirens and wondered if the ranger had a car phone. Because what was happening at this moment was no dream. This bouncing and jouncing on the metal floor of a truck was real. It hurt. Tomorrow she would have black-and-blue marks to prove it.

She wondered where she would be tomorrow—on her way home or on the last lap of her journey? She had no idea where this pickup was headed, and she dared not poke her head out to see. She smiled to herself. Like it or not, she was a turtle. She just wished she had a harder shell because the going was getting rougher. The truck had evidently turned off the main highway onto a steep road full of S turns. Finally, after clattering along a gravel road that seemed to go on forever, the truck slowed and stopped.

Sarah waited for the driver to get out. He didn't. She couldn't figure out what he was doing. Finally, she realized that he was listening to the car radio. She hoped it wasn't a news program.

At last the driver got out, slammed the door behind him and walked away, his boots crunching on gravel. Sarah made herself wait until she had counted to sixty slowly five times. Then, cautiously she peeked out.

A sign said: "Mesa Verde National Park." Tents and campers of every description were set up or parked nearby. But they seemed to be empty. There was nobody around. She soon realized why. In the center of a large clearing, a campfire glowed. Around it a great many people sat on the ground, on blankets or on folding chairs. A ranger, perhaps the driver of the truck, stood beside the fire, a guitar slung over his shoulder.

Taking her backpack and camera, Sarah got out of the truck and moved away from it as quickly as she could. She stood beside a huge Winnebago, hoping that anyone who saw her would think it was her vacation home.

The ranger was talking. The people clapped. He took up his guitar and began to play. Sarah crept closer, hugging the shadows. The music was sweet and people nodded their heads and tapped their feet as the ranger sang a song about Coyote. The song said that before the earth was finished, Coyote was so curious to see what was in the Great Creator's basket, he accidentally tipped it over scattering thousands and thousands of tiny white flowers all over the Creator's freshly painted sky. "'Oh, no, ow ow ow wow,' Coyote howled when he saw what he had done. And just so, every coyote howls to this day."

It was a long song, with many verses, and every chorus was the same. "Oh no, ow ow ow wow," the ranger sang.

"Oh no, ow ow ow wow" sounded from a dark ridge in the distance. First one and then another coyote echoed the sound.

Sarah hurried away. The ranger was doing Mother Earth's

joyful work. Sarah had a different part to play. She was sure of it now. The fact that the truck had brought her to this place, exactly where she wanted to be, within walking distance of the blue mesa, was a clear, unmistakable sign.

She set off across a rocky plain covered with knee-high grasses. Leaving the warmth and light of the campground, she headed for the dark ridge where coyotes howled. Twilight was thickening into darkness. The air was full of bats, wheeling and swooping, sometimes straight at Sarah, and then darting away at the last second. Their crazy flight pattern made her smile. She knew they meant her no harm and were actually doing her a favor as they sought their evening meal among the insects. Supper for you and fewer mosquito bites for me, she thought, wishing she had an internal radar system like a bat's to help her steer clear of hummocks and bushes which were getting harder and harder to see.

The moon would be full tonight but she was not eager for it to rise until she had crossed this exposed plain and reached the cover of the juniper forest. In the excitement of making her escape, she had not realized how tired she was.

Charlie was right. Chia seeds and trail mix were easier to carry than bread and jars of peanut butter. Her knapsack felt as if it weighed a ton and she was tempted to leave it or at least empty the heavy stuff out of it. But she didn't have a lot of trail mix and she remembered what Charlie had said about how much energy, knowledge and hard work it took to live on desert plants, especially in unknown territory. He told her that in a survival situation, insects might be a better bet. In ancient times, he said, many California tribes ate earthworms boiled in soup, and grasshoppers roasted in a kind of oven made of hot rocks. "A valuable source of protein," Charlie pointed out.

Ugh, Sara thought, and decided that heavy or not, she would lug her peanut butter. Tired and afraid to use her flashlight, she crashed through sagebrush and stumbled over rocks, although she was trying hard to flow over the land like a weasel, leaving no tracks. It would be a cinch for someone like Charlie to pick up her trail.

But there were not many trackers like Charlie. And so far, nobody seemed to know that she was here. She had to get across this open field before the campfire singalong broke up and people started looking around. She willed herself to keep going and did not stop again until she reached the trees. They grew thickly on a steep hillside and there did not seem to be a level piece of ground anywhere. But by now she was used to curling up in Mother Earth's lap, even if it was a bit rocky. In the shelter of rustling juniper branches, with her backpack as a pillow, she was asleep before moonrise.

She woke early and decided to eat her bread and peanut butter on top of the ridge where she could watch the day begin. Looking for the easiest way up, she zigzagged back and forth across the slope. The ground was strewn with wildflowers— bell-shaped orange and yellow blossoms of mariposa lily, brilliant red Indian paintbrush and cardinal monkeyflower. She walked carefully to avoid crushing them and sometimes bent down to admire their delicate beauty. Rested and fresh, she did not dawdle, but she did not rush, either. It was as if sleeping on the bare earth last night had reunited her with the natural world in which time is an eternal circle not an agonizing race to beat a ticking clock. Steadily, she climbed, moving through groves of pinyon and juniper and gambel oak. Scrub jays and towhees sat on branches and called good morning to each other, to her, to the world in general. Warblers flitted about like butterflies while tiny nuthatches made their way up and down tree trunks with jerky motions like wind-up toys.

Suddenly the land simply stopped, fell off into nothingness. What she had thought was a ridge with a gently sloping far side, ended in a a cliff so high that swallows and ravens wheeled below. Stretching to the horizon were huge, table-like mesas with green foliage topping them like tablecloths. Between the mesas were deep canyons with sheer rock walls. On these mesas and in caves in these canyon walls, Mama had told her, the ancients built their homes, raised their children, worshiped their gods, and looked at the same view Sarah was looking at now. As far as Sarah could see, there was not a house or a road or a fence. There was just the land, lonely and majestic, wild and free, as the Great Creator made it. She stood there for a long time, utterly alone and utterly happy.

Finally, she sat down, to eat and drink dreamily with her eyes fixed on the view that was constantly changing as the sun rose.

Then she saw it. Why not before? Had the light changed? Had she shifted her gaze? Who could say? But there it was. A blue mesa. Ship-shaped like the others, pointing in the same direction, but different because its tabletop was not one of the many shades of green. It was blue. Unmistakably blue.

Alone, with no one to see, Sarah jumped up and did a little dance. A victory dance. The end of her journey was in sight.

When she calmed down, she stared hard at the blue mesa. There was no sign of a cave or a ruin in its cliff wall. But she had no doubt that a cliff house with five square rooms and a kiva was over there somewhere. She had found the blue mesa. She would find the cliff house, too. Maybe before nightfall. Maybe before noon.

She reminded herself that in the desert, distances deceive. The blue mesa might be a lot nearer or a lot farther away than it looked. But it was early. The day was still cool. There was a light breeze and a few clouds in the sky. A good day for hiking. And she had never felt better in her life.

It took a while for her to find a way down the cliff. It was not a real trail but the path of a rockslide so ancient that its boulders were firmly embedded forming a staircase for giants. Not being a giant, Sarah had trouble getting from one level to another. Each descent was a puzzle to solve. Sometimes she crawled. Sometimes she hung by her hands and dropped six or eight feet onto a rock shelf. Sometimes she simply sat down and slid. Bad for the blue jeans, but fast.

By noon, she was on the valley floor among scrubby little trees and small-leaved bushes. In the sandier places, there were grasses and cacti. But Charlie had taught her that unlike the cottonwoods, these tough little trees and bushes could survive on the occasional runoff of rain from the mesa tops. Their presence didn't necessarily mean that there was water nearby. So she decided that if she didn't find water, she would turn back when the first of her two water bottles was empty. In the meantime, she would be careful to drink at least a cupful every hour. Thirst muddled the brain and she couldn't afford that. She was alone. She had to make her own decisions. And she needed to be alert enough to find water if there was any around.

Need sharpened her senses. She saw everything and sensed much that she did not see. The rustle of a lizard. The drift of needles under a dead juniper. An anthill. And, late in the day, footprints. Although she could not read the land the way Charlie could, she recognized the heart-shaped prints of many mule deer and the leaf-shaped prints of a coyote, going in the same direction, across the sand, toward a pile of boulders in the distance. Without hesitation, Sarah followed the tracks. If coyote and deer were heading straight for the same place, it was not to kill or be killed. It was for the one thing that could persuade them to declare a temporary truce. Water.

She found it in a tiny spring surrounded by sandstone boulders. Rain-water, pure and sweet. When she had satisfied her thirst and refilled her water bottle, she rested on a rock nearby, camera in hand to see who else would come to drink. She was about to give up when a pair of doves came and perched companionably side by side on the edge of the little pool. She aimed her camera at them but as she pressed the shutter, they flew away. Something had startled them. What?

Could the camera be quicker than the eye? Mama thought so.

When Sarah set off once more, she marked her way with small stone towers so that she could find this rain-filled basin again, if need be.

Now the light little breeze, which had faded at noon, freshened. Occasionally a cloud drifted across the sun. What a pleasant land this was. No wonder the Anasazi built their homes here. Why did they ever leave?

She reached the foot of the blue mesa at dusk. A flash of bright green caught her eye. Maidenhair fern and wild grape leaves were growing on a tiny ledge. Behind them the rock was wet. Water was seeping from a crack in the canyon wall and falling down, one tiny droplet at a time, onto the ledge. It would take hours to fill a water bottle from this hidden spring. But there were no clocks here. Nature and Sarah could afford to be patient. She propped her open water bottle on the ledge under the dripping crack and settled down for the night. How uncomplicated life was in the wilderness. She spread her groundcloth, unlaced

her boots, ate another peanut butter sandwich, drank some water and went to sleep. She did not see the moon rise or hear the great horned owl hooting softly in the distance.

The next morning she realized how exhausted she had been the night before. She had carelessly left her camera out and had knocked it over in her sleep. Checking it, she saw that the shutter had been tripped, accidentally taking the last picture on the roll. Luckily, she had another. She reloaded the camera, ate some trail mix, retrieved her water bottle which was full to the brim, and went to look for a way up the cliff.

It was late afternoon before she found a trail. Well, it began as a trail but halfway up it turned into toe and fingerholds chipped out of the rock. Placing her feet and hands carefully in the niches and not daring to look down, Sarah climbed thirty feet to a small ledge. From here she could see the ruin of the

Anasazi village at the mouth of a wide and high cave that curved back like a gigantic bandshell.

The light was fading but the long shadows would make an interesting photograph. As the shutter clicked, Sarah had the feeling that something moved away, retreated, melted into the shadows. But she saw nothing and she knew that only in her imagination could she see what she wanted most to see. But here, in this spirit-filled place, the vision of that beloved face was clearer than it had ever been. "I'm here, Mama," she whispered. "I'm here. And life is as beautiful as you said it could be."

Sarah climbed up and over a rocky stretch that led to a wider ledge that must have been easy walking long ago. Working her way around a mass of fallen rock and juniper branches, Sarah entered the vast cave. The rock walls shut out every sound— birdsong, wind, the rustle of leaves. It was like walking into a cathedral. In the immense silence, there were only two sounds: Sarah's footsteps and the faint, faraway, life-giving sound of falling water.

In the last of the daylight Sarah explored the cave. She found walls made of rocks that had been shaped by human hands seven hundred years ago. She saw the black smoke marks of a thousand fires. She found an old mortar and a heap of chipped stone left from making spearheads. She traced the outline of five rooms and a kiva, each one totally, terribly empty, silently asking the question. Why, when, where did the people go?

Did it matter? Perhaps it did. Perhaps it was important
to know that whole civilizations could disappear
if the water ran out or the soil blew away
or factories polluted the crystal air.

She traced the murmuring water to its source, a spring at the back of the cave. The ancients had built a low wall around the spring so that the water formed a little pool and was easy to dip up. Near the spring lay a broken bowl of black-and-white pottery. Walking carefully in case there were more pottery pieces around, Sarah filled her water bottle, and went back to look at the kiva again.

Most of its encircling wall remained standing, but the roof had caved in and poles and fallen rock half-filled the sunken circle. But the fire pit was clear and so was the *sipapu*, the small hole in the dirt floor that all kivas had because the Anasazi believed that their ancestors had come into this world from a world below. A strange idea, Sarah had thought when she first heard it. Now she wondered if it seemed strange only because it was like heaven, an idea you couldn't really put into words.

A wide bench ran completely around the inner wall of the kiva, and the plaster of every interior surface was glowing a dusty rose color. Suddenly Sarah was seized with a desire to spend the night in the kiva. She set her backpack on the wide, smooth, rose colored bench. Had her mother sat there? Was it this kiva she wanted Sarah to see? Or the birds and animals and plants she had passed on the way? Or a way of life?

Before the sun went down, she gathered tinder and made a fire and heated a can of spaghetti she had sneaked into her pack when Charlie wasn't looking. Odd to be heating canned spaghetti on a fire made with a fire board and drill. She was living in two worlds. And it was possible to love them both. For a long time she sat at the entrance to the cave, looking out at the night sky where stars glittered separately and in clusters and sometimes sailed in wide-winging arcs. Shooting stars. Stars to wish on. But the moment was perfect. Even a wish, Sarah thought, might spoil it.

•11•

The sky was a bright, perfect blue the next morning when Sarah went out to look around. She carried her camera and her backpack. She had been tempted to leave the backpack in the kiva because she planned to be gone for only a few minutes but the memory of Charlie's stern voice rang in her ears. "Carry it." She sighed. Making yourself do things you don't want to do is hard, but when you do them, it feels good.

At the rim of a small side canyon, the ledge she was following turned into a narrow trail. She had considered climbing to the top of the mesa but at every point above her there seemed to be only sheer cliffs and dangerous overhangs. The trail was an animal trail and the creatures that used it were more interested in tender leaves and succulent grass than in getting to the top of anything. So the trail wandered this way and that along the side of the mesa at more or less the same level for quite a distance. Fine, Sarah thought. She had two photographs to take and there were wonderful views everywhere.

Overhead a golden eagle circled higher and higher until it disappeared. This lord of the sky was not about to sit to have his photograph taken. But a few minutes later, a deep *hoo-hoo-hoo* sounded from a juniper tree. Sarah looked, and staring back at her were the round yellow eyes of a great horned owl. Rigid, white lines drawn down between the eyes, ear tufts sticking up like little horns, the bird looked indignant. What about me, it seemed to be saying. Am I not the largest owl? Am I not found

everywhere in North America up to the northern tree limit? Am I not a superb hunter? You'd be overrun with rats and mice if you didn't have owls. And I am the king of the owls.

Sarah moved in close and took a photograph. The great horned owl did not move a feather, did not even blink. Only one more picture to take. She should be overjoyed. She could go home now, and she wanted to, but she knew that a time like this might never come again. Her life at home had been busy and would only get busier. She would grow up. She would never again be quite this free.

The trail was sloping upward now, looping around rocky outcroppings, luring her on with butterflies—tigertails, white skippers, small blues and painted ladies with their salmon-orange wings black-bordered and blue-spotted as if dressed for the fanciest party in the world. Kneeling to photograph them, she felt as if she could enter their world, a dream world of airy, carefree flight. A bend in the trail told her that the real world was harsher than that.

The carcass of a mule deer lay in a sandy hollow. Fresh, still bloody, it had already been torn apart and, in places, stripped to bare bone. The lifeless heap lay so close to the trail that she might have stepped on it. She forced herself to look carefully, to examine the earth around the dead creature. A number of animal tracks converged on the kill. Coyote. But he had come later, to eat the leftovers. The mark of the killer was unmistakable. Rounded pawmarks. Four toes up front, four in the rear, without claws. Neat, delicate and huge. Striding, stalking and then, without pause, bounding in for the kill. It was all there written in the sand. Mountain lion. Cougar. Puma. Devil cat. They said there was one in Magic Canyon, but she had never seen it and her father said it might be only a legend.

But this mountain lion was real. It was also, quite possibly, nearby. It could be ahead of her on the trail coming back for second helpings. Time to go. She turned and retraced her steps but before she was ten feet away from the carcass, brown-black wings descended. Turkey vulture. The clean-up crew.

When she reached the overhang that sheltered the cliff house, Sarah stopped in a patch of sunlight to drink some water and think about the mule deer. Nothing lived forever. Not in the same form. Only man refused to accept that. Idly she ran her fingers over the rock wall behind her. Even mountains crumbled into dust. She whirled around to see what her fingers were telling her. The dust she was feeling lay in a chipped-out indentation in the rock. And there was more: footholds and handholds leading up the face of the cliff to a flat rocky area above. She put her camera and water bottle in her backpack, slipped its straps over her shoulders, and began to climb. When the top of her head was almost level with the rock shelf, her face pressed close to the warm, orange rock wall, she smelled it: a sharp, acrid, animal smell. Cat. Ancient, nameless fear seized her, blood pounded in her ears. On the edge of panic, she ordered herself not to move a muscle, not to breathe, willing her aching hands to hang on, praying that the rock she was clinging to would not give way. A huge yellow shape blocked her view of the sky and then a long, tawny body hurtled clear over her head, landed lightly on the ledge below and strolled casually into the cliff house.

With shaking hands, Sarah climbed onto the rock shelf above her, where the mountain lion had been minutes before. He must have been heading home after a night of hunting. Had he seen her, smelled her? Did he know that she had slept in his cave? Probably. But the mule deer was his kill and he had eaten his fill. Now he would drink from the spring in the cliff house, stretch his strong, lithe body, and sleep.

Sarah took a deep breath and a drink of water, and turned her attention to the cliff wall above her. She was looking for a continuation of the trail. If she could get to the top of the mesa, she might be able to see another route down, one that did not lead past the front door of a two-hundred-pound mountain lion who might be losing patience with her.

Now that she knew what to look for, she found it quickly. A few chipped niches led to a long, diagonal crease in the rock.

For the Anasazi, with their tough bare feet, this narrow crease would have been as good as a highway. Sarah, light and agile, with small feet and good boots, inched her way up. She did not think about falling. She did not think about reaching the top. Every ounce of her attention was concentrated on where and how to place her feet and hands for the next step.

When she came to the top of the mesa, she found that she could not cross it because the way was blocked by a towering rock formation. Her heart sank.

Then she thought of Broken Knife Canyon, remembering how disappointed she had been when it appeared that Silver Woman River had dried up. She had panicked and would have given up but Charlie had calmly continued to search. Shading her eyes with her hand, she studied the rock, trying to read its secrets.

Mama said all rocks had secrets. Geodes hid rainbows and roses in their hearts. Slabs of shale hid fault lines ready to release catastrophic landslides. What appeared to be a solid rock might have succumbed to the relentless carving of water tunneling a way through. She remembered the crack between the boulders in Magic Canyon, the secret pass she and Mama called the lemon squeezer. A stranger would walk right by it, never noticing it. She turned her attention to the gigantic rock wall, slowly and painstakingly examining it, inch by inch. If there was a way through, she would find it if it took all day.

Again and again, she came upon what appeared to be a tunnel or a pass, only to come to a dead end. It was getting hard to keep her hopes up. But, she told herself, that was not the point. The point was to continue to investigate every possibility before she quit. She'd be a pile of bleached bones in Broken Knife Canyon if she had given up when she thought she had reached her limit.

Almost an hour later, she saw an opening in the rocks, a shallow cave so low she would have to get down on her hands and knees to investigate it. It looked exactly like all the other holes she had been crawling into. Dead ends, all of them, as this was sure to be, too. Her back ached and her hands were covered with scratches, but she made herself crawl into the hole. Shining her flashlight ahead of her, she saw that it was a tunnel, a low, narrow one, too dark to be promising but she had to check it out. Rubble hurt her knees, and the roof of the tunnel kept getting lower and lower. A bad sign. Still she went on. Finally, she stopped. The beam of her flashlight was playing on a rock wall that blocked the tunnel thirty feet ahead. Her heart sank but she was also relieved. There was no way through. She could quit looking.

But something Charlie said about going the distance made her pause. Until she actually touched that rock wall, she could not turn back. Her body had other ideas. It began to shake with fatigue. Thirty feet seemed like thirty miles. But when she reached it, she discovered that the rock wall was not the end of the tunnel. It was a corner. The tunnel turned right, widened, got higher, and ran uphill like a ramp. Soon Sarah could stand, walk, and when she saw daylight ahead, she almost ran.

She came out into a blue world. Bluer than sky. Bluer than water. Pale blue. Deep rich blue. Blue-gray. Blue violet. From one

end to the other, as far as she could see, the top of the mesa was carpeted with blue flowers. Miles of lupine in every shade of blue, slender, erect, like tall blue candles, glowed in the afternoon sun.

So it was not a trick of light, not dark shadows on junipers. The mesa really was blue. But only when the lupine was in bloom. Had she come earlier in the year or later, she might have looked right at Blue Mesa and never recognized it. She might not have found the Anasazi ruin, might not have been able to finish her task. It seemed like a miracle. Her father would call it coincidence. What was the difference? Was there any?

Happily, Sarah drifted through the waving blue field to the far edge of the mesa. The view was much the same. More canyons, more flat-topped rock tables. But on this side, the drop to the

canyon floor was gradual. A trail led off to the right. It looked like a horse trail. Unlike goat trails, horse trails led to people. She moved along the edge of the mesa in an effort to see where the trail led. But she was looking too far into the distance. When she began scanning the land close to the foot of the mesa, she saw a house, a barn and a fenced field almost directly below.

Suddenly, she wanted desperately to be there. She saw herself walking up to the house. May I use your telephone? Hello, Daddy? She heard her father's voice. Tears filled her eyes. She wanted to be home. To be playing Monopoly on the kitchen table. To be eating chocolate chip ice cream. To sleep in her own bed.

She hurried down the trail, almost unaware of her surroundings. She had already reentered the world she had left only a

week ago. A world where the past and the future distracted her from the present. Had she been as alert as she had been only a few hours ago, she would have heard the horse before it loomed up in front of her. Startled, she let out a little cry. The rider, a young girl who appeared to be about Sarah's age, reined the horse in. "Hi," she said. "I'm Elena Lopez. Who are you?"

"I'm Sarah Stewart."

Elena's eyes widened. "The lost girl?"

"I'm not lost," Sarah said, "but I would like to use your telephone."

After that things happened fast, so fast that looking back Sarah saw only scenes, blurring and overlapping. The Lopez house. The airport. Her father coming toward her, holding out his arms. The flight home. Home. Meetings with the police and Corey Blake and Charlie Night and a lot of other people. Answering questions. In one scene, Sarah saw herself, confused and outnumbered, asking if it would be all right if she asked Charlie Night a question.

"Of course."

"When was the very first time you saw me?"

"A few minutes ago when you walked into the room."

Sarah looked puzzled but said nothing. Her father looked relieved. On the flight home, she had poured out in a breathlessly excited jumble every detail of her journey, had told him about Broken Knife Canyon, had told him about Charlie, had wanted to know how he could be in two places at once. Her father had listened calmly, holding her hand. "Don't worry about it, sweetheart," he had said. "You've been through a lot. In a few days, it will all fall into place."

•12•

In a way, Sarah decided, her father was right. A week later, her adventures in Broken Knife Canyon and on Blue Mesa had taken on a dreamlike quality, as if they had happened in another life. Now familiarity surrounded her, absorbed her, shut everything else out. She was setting the table. Her father was making biscuits. Chili was bubbling on the stove. And the phone had finally stopped ringing.

But she was still curious about Charlie. "I don't see how he could have been with you and Corey and everybody the whole time he was with me."

"Honey," her father said gently, "you only imagined that Charlie was with you."

"Why would I do that?"

"It's a common phenomenon. A natural reaction to isolation, lack of food and water, sleep deprivation. Anyone who spent a week in the desert, alone, the way you did, might hear voices and see a mirage."

"But Charlie was real. He looked and acted and talked like a real person."

"Well, you have a vivid imagination."

"And he didn't just appear and disappear like a mirage. He stayed with me and watched over me like a guardian spirit."

"Well, that's what he was, then—your guardian spirit. And I'm grateful to him—or it—for keeping you safe."

"Will we see him again?"

"Sure. Next week, in fact. Steve Karloff wants Charlie and you to testify at the Magic Canyon hearing and he's scheduled a strategy meeting on the eleventh. I'll pick you up right after school."

At three-thirty on the eleventh, Sarah and her father and Charlie Night were sitting in a downtown law office waiting for Steve Karloff to emerge from behind a closed door with his name on it. Instead, a secretary came into the waiting room to say that Mr. Karloff had been unavoidably delayed.

Charlie looked up, nodded and said nothing. Gerald Stewart thanked her and opened a magazine. Sarah took a deep breath and asked Charlie if he would talk to her about guardian spirits. She said she had read about them in books but the stories were always about Indians who lived many years ago. Did spirit helpers appear to Native Americans today? And did they always take the form of an animal or a snake or a fish or a bird?

Charlie laughed. "Ask me about rocks," he said. "I know more about geology and petroglyphs than I do about the spirit world."

"But you're studying with a famous medicine man."

"I've just begun. I have a lot to learn."

"But you know more than I do. Please."

"All right. Guardian spirits have traditionally appeared mostly in animal form, probably because for hundreds of years Native American people and animals have lived together in the wilderness in close harmony. It's natural that our four-legged brothers, our winged sisters would respond to the love and respect we bear for them. But I have heard of spirit helpers appearing in human form—as wise old men or mystic warriors. Even as a beautiful woman in a rainbow shawl." He stopped and raised his eyebrows. "Anything else you want to know?"

"Yes," Sarah said. "What would you do if I told you that you were a guardian spirit—my guardian spirit on my difficult and dangerous journey?"

"I would respect your vision."

"But would you say that it is true or not true?"

"I would say that it is true for you. Because that is what my grandmother taught me. That is what William Songchanter says. 'Respect your brothers' and sisters' visions.' Trouble comes

when we try to make everyone see what we see, believe what
we believe. The Great Mystery reveals itself in small, shining
fragments, each one true but light years away from the
Infinite Whole."

Sarah looked at her father. He had stopped reading. He had
been listening. He took her hand and smiled. She smiled back.
After all, hadn't it been her father who had called Charlie her
guardian spirit and said he was grateful to him—or it—for
keeping her safe?

A few minutes later, Steve Karloff arrived and explained the
legal game plan. He said that he planned to ask both Sarah and
Charlie to speak on behalf of Magic Canyon. He said they were
not to worry about scientific graphs, charts and statistics on the
fragility of desert ecosystems. He had scientists to present this
data, and he himself would make the opening statement. At
some point, he would ask Charlie to present the Indian view of
the earth as sacred ground where all living things are related. At
the end, Sarah would ask the officials and all people everywhere
to save wild places for their children and their grandchildren.

Before her journey, Sarah would have been terrified at the
idea of getting up and making a speech in court. Now she knew
she could do harder things than that. And she had her photographs. The lawyer said that if she could not find the right
words, the pictures would tell the story. All she really had to do
was to hold them up. One at a time. Not too quickly. Give the
audience time to study them. To see that in the wilderness there
are many things we overlook. Tiny plants and animals we don't
notice. Powerful forces just out of sight. It is important, the
lawyer would tell the audience, to consider both the seen and
the unseen.

The hearing was held in a large courtroom but every specta-
tor seat was filled. Standing was not allowed so people gathered
in clumps in the hallways, along with reporters and cameramen.

Corey Blake was there and Sarah waved to him as she came
in. Since her return, he had been working on a major article

about desert canyons and the need to save them. He said he didn't want to write a routine conservation piece. He was trying to make people understand the idea of living in harmony with the earth. For an article like that to get published, Corey said, it had to have news value and human interest. Sarah's journey had both. When he talked to her about it, he hadn't asked a lot of silly questions. And unlike other people who asked about her journey, he was interested not only in what had happened but in what Sarah thought and felt and how her thoughts and feelings changed as she moved away from civilization. She was even able to talk to him about Charlie being her guardian spirit. He seemed genuinely interested. He said he understood what Einstein meant when he said, "The more knowledge we acquire, the more mystery we find."

As for the spirit world, Corey said, if your definition of it was broad enough to include courage and kindness, hope and love, it was a heck of a lot more powerful than the material world.

Sitting in the courtroom with her father on one side and Charlie on the other, Sarah was amazed at the size of the crowd. "I never dreamed there would be this many people," she said.

"We need them," her father said. "In the end, one way or another, it's the people who decide what kind of a world we're going to have."

Steve Karloff began, showing his charts, hammering his points home. Charlie spoke next, of native wisdom and lost joy and a way of living that could still be relearned. He spoke of walking softly on the earth and leaving it unharmed when you depart.

Finally, Sarah held her pictures up. The audience murmured. She heard the words "beautiful," "wonderful." The City Council members listened attentively to what she had to say about the children, how cramped and sad their lives would be without wild places, rippling streams, fields of blue lupine and the call of the great horned owl. "The earth is my mother," Sarah said, "and your mother, too. She loves you and needs you. Please be kind to her."

At the conclusion of the hearing, the Mayor said that the council would meet in closed session in the afternoon and would announce their decision tomorrow morning at nine.

"You got it made, kid," Corey Blake said to Sarah as he rushed past her toward the phones.

Steve Karloff said, "You were very effective, young lady. Nice job, Charlie. I hope they got the message. I have a plane to catch. We'll be in touch."

In the hall people crowded around Sarah congratulating her on her beautiful pictures and asking questions about her journey. For the most part they seemed disappointed with her answers.

"What did you do about rattlesnakes?"

"I didn't see any."

"Did you kill the mountain lion?"

"Why should I? And how could I?"

"Are you going to have an exhibit of the pottery and the other artifacts you brought back?"

"I didn't bring anything back."

Except, she wanted to add, memories of an adventure I wish everyone could have.

"Have lunch with us, Charlie," Mr. Stewart said. He turned to Sarah. "Where shall we go?"

Sarah looked at Charlie. "Pizza Plaza?"

"Right on."

There were fewer people at the courthouse the next morning. Those who were merely curious had seen what they had come to see—the runaway girl and the Indian. But others came early, as Sarah and her father did, eager to hear the verdict. Singly and in groups, they waited for the doors to open. Charlie introduced Sarah to some of the members of the Badger Society, and a new group, that called itself Citizens Concerned About Canyons, asked her to join. The president was a young woman in her thirties. She said that her father had been a mayor and she had grown up vowing never to have anything to do with politics. "So many good causes are lost," she told Sarah. "I wasn't brave enough to fail. But when I heard what you were doing, I knew I had to at least try."

It was over in five minutes. The City Council filed in. The mayor announced their decision. The vote was five to four against the proposal to acquire Magic Canyon for a wildlife preserve. The City Council filed out. There was a smattering of applause. Someone murmured about construction equalling jobs. But most of the audience sat in startled silence. It had been such a good show, a full-court press, pictures, an Indian, a kid. They had to win. But they lost.

"Come on, honey," Mr. Stewart said, taking Sarah's hand and leading her out of the building, down the courthouse steps and into the car. He drove in silence, out of town, into the desert where he parked in the shade of Creation Mountain and took his daughter in his arms.

For a long time he let her cry. Then, because he never carried a handkerchief, he offered her his shirttail to dry her eyes. She couldn't help laughing at that although tears were still running down her face. "How could they do that?" she said. "Why?"

"Money," her father said. "To preserve Magic Canyon in its wild state, the town would have to buy it. To do that, they would have to borrow money and raise taxes to pay it back. Those are elected officials. They want to keep their jobs and they know you don't get re-elected by raising taxes. But look, sweetheart, you did well to get the hearing. It got a lot of people interested in the cause."

So many good causes are lost, that young woman had said in the courthouse hall this morning. But Sarah had hoped so much and tried so hard. She had been brave, faced hardship and danger. But nothing on her journey had been harder to face than this.

When Sarah and her father got home a car was parked in front of the house. When he heard them drive up, Corey Blake got out and handed Sarah a bunch of wildflowers including blue lupine. It was tied with blue ribbon, and tucked in among the blossoms was a card that said: "In deepest sympathy."

"I really am sorry," Corey said.

"I know you are," Sarah said. "Thank you."

"Would you like to come in?" Mr. Stewart asked.

Corey said he would, but just for a few minutes. He had a favor to ask. Would Sarah consider letting him use her photographs in his article? The magazine would pay for them, of course, and give her credit.

"You still want to do the article?" Sarah asked.

"Of course."

"But we lost."

"A battle. Not the war. The earth's still got a lot of wild places to save."

Mr. Stewart poured coffee and Sarah went for the photographs. Corey examined each one carefully and asked Sarah where and when it was taken.

When Sarah asked him which prints he wanted to use, he said he'd like to take them all so that the art director could make the selection.

Sarah said fine, what else was she going to do with them?

At the door Corey said, "Don't hold your breath waiting for this article to come out. It will take a couple of weeks at least."

They said good-bye and Corey went out to his car. Two minutes later he was back. "Reporters are pests," he said, "but I wonder if you have a picture of yourself. I really need one for the article. I could send a photographer out but that would mean more delay."

Sarah thought for a minute. She certainly didn't want him using her fifth-grade class picture. In that stupid dress with that bored look on her face. She went into her bedroom and came out with her favorite photograph, one her mother had taken of her in Magic Canyon in early spring when the water was high. "Please don't lose it," Sarah said. "I think we have the negative somewhere but I'm not sure."

Corey promised to take care of the photograph, said good-bye and drove off.

So it was all over, Sarah thought. Time for a big banner saying THE END. But there could be no applause. The bulldozers would roll again. Fan palms would fall. Water would be led into captivity. But life would go on. Mr. Stewart would fix the back porch and Sarah would get new shoes and start sixth grade.

The wildflowers Corey had brought lay on the table. Sarah picked them up and put them in a blue pitcher. How beautiful that mesa had been. She would never forget it.

"I suppose they'll be out there digging up Magic Canyon tomorrow," she said. No, her father told her, construction could not start quite that fast. The archaeological study had turned up shell money and pottery shards. Their find was limited to a small area, roughly fifty feet square. But it meant that the whole development plan would have to be redrawn.

"It doesn't change the court decision," Mr. Stewart said. "It does buy us a little more time to enjoy Magic Canyon in its wild state. I think we ought to do that."

Sarah hesitated. Saying good-bye to the canyon would be sad, but as long as she could, she had to visit it. So they went together with bedrolls and supplies and spent the night. It was like a homecoming. Memories, hundreds of them, filled the air like bright butterflies. At every turn of the trail, Sarah met herself, sometimes alone, sometimes with her mother. Everything they had done, everything they had seen, every animal, bird, insect, leaf, flower, sunrise, sunset was a memory she could take away and keep forever.

This camping trip with her father would be a memory some day. Perhaps that was why he had suggested it. Her journey had taught them both that Sarah would soon be grown up, changed, different and, in a way, gone. Her father needed memories, too.

•13•

They were in Magic Canyon, sitting on a boulder with their feet in the water, when Sarah asked her father a question that surprised him. "Do you think Grandma and Grandpa Stewart still want me to come to visit them?"

"Of course."

"And you want to go, don't you?"

"Very much. But this has been a tough year for you and I don't want to ask you to do something you don't want to do."

"It wasn't that I didn't want to go," Sarah said. "I couldn't go before because I had to try to save Magic Canyon. I was needed here. Now I'm not."

So they went east to the sea and did all the things Sarah's father had done when he was a child. They swam, sailed, fished, picked beach plums, went out on a lobster boat, and slept in a house where there was no radio or television, only the endless sound of the sea.

A week before school opened, Sarah and her father flew home. She had loved the blue-green ocean, the yellow-green marsh, the floating veils of fog, but at first sight of the dry, harsh, rock-strewn, thorny, unforgiving desert, her heart began to sing. She was home.

As they walked through the door, the phone began to ring. Sarah ran to pick it up. It was Corey Blake. "Where've you been?" he asked.

"On Cape Cod. With my grandparents."

"What did they think? Did it knock their socks off?"

[166]

"What?"

"That Mother Earth thing. Everybody's been calling me about it."

"What Mother Earth thing?"

"Are you kidding me, Sarah?"

"No."

"You mean you haven't seen it?"

"Seen what?"

"*Newsview!*"

"Oh, your story. I'm sorry, Corey. I forgot about it. We didn't see a newspaper or magazine or watch television the whole time we were away. I hope my pictures look good. We'll get a copy of the magazine tomorrow when we go for the mail."

"Better bring a moving van," Corey said.

"What for?"

"For your mail."

Sarah laughed. "Like I have a lot of boyfriends or something?"

"Like for once I'm not kidding," Corey said. "You'd better let me talk to your father."

Corey talked and Mr. Stewart listened, his eyebrows going up in surprise. Occasionally he said, "Really?" Finally he said, "We sure would, but we can wait. Oh, I see. Fine! See you soon."

"Corey's in town," Mr. Stewart said to Sarah. "He's coming out to the house."

"Now?"

"Yes."

"To show us the magazine article?"

"Yes."

"Great. I wonder how many photographs the magazine used."

"I gather quite a few. Corey says a lot has been happening. He wants to tell us about it. He says it will knock our socks off."

Sarah laughed. "He always says that."

Corey Blake arrived with a pint of chocolate chip ice cream, a stack of *Newsview* magazines and all of Sarah's photographs.

The picture of Sarah that her mother had taken in the canyon was in a separate envelope marked: "Return to Owner on Pain of Death."

"I took good care of it," Corey told her, handing it over.

"I knew you would," she said.

Corey and Mr. Stewart chatted while Sarah went to put the ice cream in the freezer and then to her bedroom to return the photograph to its frame. She was glad to have it back. The room looked right again.

Her life was beginning to look right again, too. She could talk to Daddy now the way she used to talk to Mama. And he could talk to her about the things that were close to his heart. About Grandpa Stewart's failing eyesight and the storm damage to the barrier beach that protected the driftwood cottage. Now, as she stood in the half-dark bedroom, it occurred to Sarah that growing up could mean growing closer, not growing away. She had an impulse to run and tell her father but suddenly she was quite sure he knew.

"Okay, kid," Corey said when Sarah came back into the living room. "Open your hands and close your eyes and I'll give you something that'll knock your socks off." Sarah did as she was told, felt the glossy paper in her hands, opened her eyes and stared at the cover of *Newsview*.

For a long, long time, she said nothing. Then she said very softly, "The earth is my mother."

The picture on the cover of the magazine was impossible to explain but it explained everything. Hundreds of thousands of people writing, phoning, sending telegrams to congressmen and senators, to the Department of the Interior, to the Bureau of Land Management, the Forestry Department, the National Park Service, the governor, the president, to demand that Magic Canyon be preserved. Sending money, an avalanche of money, to a foundation set up and jointly administered by Citizens Concerned About Canyons and the Badger Society—enough money for the foundation to buy back Magic Canyon and guarantee its wildness forever.

"Does Charlie know?" Sarah asked Corey.

"Of course. He helped organize the foundation. He's on the board. He's been trying to reach you. He called my office half a dozen times but I didn't know where you were either. You should have left the answering machine on. On second thought, it's a good thing you didn't. It would have broken down under the load. Seems like every organization in the country wants you to come and speak to them. Girl Scouts. Garden Club. Rocky Mountain Hiking Club. Rotary."

"Rotary?" Mr. Stewart asked.

"Yeah, well, the Magic Canyon buyback involved having the developer take over a low-cost housing project that was going bankrupt. The foundation persuaded the bank to make the deal attractive and there was enough cash to get the thing going again so now everybody's happy. It's a real win-win situation. Jobs, housing for the poor, profit for the developer and a gorgeous hunk of nature saved from destruction."

Mr. Stewart shook his head. "It's hard to take it all in."

"But you haven't heard it all," Corey said. "There's more."

Mr. Stewart held up his hand. "Time out," he said. "I think we need an ice cream break."

Dishing up the ice cream, Sarah was so excited she fairly danced around the kitchen. Magic Canyon was safe. The palms and the brittlebush, Badger, Cougar Rock and the secret cave and the four-winged dragonflies making rainbows over the second waterfall. All safe. Forever.

When Sarah came in with the ice cream, Mr. Stewart was asking Corey why a magazine cover could move so many people to do so much.

"I think it's because they were already moved," Corey said thoughtfully. "You know, when Sarah disappeared, her story was in every newspaper and magazine and on radio and television. The whole country wondered where she was, worried about her, prayed for her and breathed a sigh of relief when she turned up safe. When they learned why she made that incredible journey, their hearts were touched. For a child to love the earth so much, it made them feel that they should be helping the earth, too. But they didn't see what Magic Canyon had to do with the parts of the earth *they* knew and loved. In my article, I tried to explain that life is a sacred circle, that everything in nature is connected. But it's hard—maybe impossible—to put into words. Then this magic happened with the cover and the pieces just fell into place and, well, people just saw."

"Why do you call it magic?" Mr. Stewart asked.

"Because it was an accident. The art director was going to use one photograph for the cover. He was having a hard time making up his mind about which one to choose. At the last minute, he decided to use them all. He just lined them up more or less as they came to hand. And suddenly, there it was. The whole story in one image. Like magic."

When they finished their ice cream, Corey said that to write his article, he had done a lot of research on the Broken Knife Canyon area. "That mine shaft you fell into," he told Sarah, "was abandoned a long time ago because the gold ran out. At some point, the government acquired the land and put the mineral rights up for sale. No takers, of course, and nobody really expected any. But times changed and helicopters began flying into canyons and gold wasn't the only thing that they were looking for. I discovered that a private mining company was trying to buy the old Broken Knife mine for its uranium deposits. When my article came out, people everywhere rose up objecting to the sale. To make a long story short, the sale's off and Broken Knife Mine is no longer up for grabs."

It was late when Corey Blake got up to go. At the door, he stopped. "Hey, Sarah," he said. "Remember Mr. Lopez?"

"Of course. Elena's father. He drove me to the airport to meet Daddy."

"Turns out the blue mesa is on his land. Or was. He's donated it to a conservation trust. What a story. Doesn't it just knock your socks off?"

When they had closed the door on Corey Blake, Sarah and her father stood staring at each other in amazement. Then they laughed and laughed and hugged and hugged. Finally, Mr. Stewart said, "Well, what now? It's considerably past your bed-time and we've had a busy day."

Sarah said she would never be able to sleep now. She was too excited. Her father said she could unpack and read for a while. She took her suitcase and the package of photographs to her bedroom. She set the suitcase down in front of the closet. Unpacking could wait. She wanted to try something.

She took the photographs out of the package and laid them out, faceup, on the top of her dresser. She examined each photo carefully. There did seem to be a relationship between them. She began to lay them out in rows, switching them around again and again, trying to get them to form that beautiful

$3.00 • *newsview.com*

August 15

NEWSVIEW

Sarah Stewart's Photos Reveal Mother Earth

image, that magical portrait that had astonished and moved so many people. She tried and tried but no matter how she arranged the photographs, the image was incomplete. She counted the photos. Fifteen. She had taken fifteen photographs on her journey. What was missing?

She sighed, and looking up, her gaze was attracted by the glint of a silver frame. Carefully she removed the photograph from the frame. She had the answer.

For a long time, Sarah stared at the beautiful face. Her mother. Not Abigail Stewart, but her other mother, the mother of us all. Mother Earth.

Finally, she turned the light out and went to the window to look out at the lovely, lonely stretches of sagebrush and cactus and hard-baked sand, at the dark silhouette of Creation Mountain and over it all, the immense blue-black desert sky.

"Sarah," her father said from the doorway, "I have an idea."

She turned.

"Would you like to spend tonight in Magic Canyon? We've said a lot of good-byes there. I thought you might like to say hello."

·14·

Washington, D.C.—At a ceremony held today in the White House Rose Garden, the president of the United States presented the first Eco Hero award to Sarah Star Stewart, age eleven. The new public service award was created to recognize individuals who have made great personal effort to protect wilderness areas and preserve them as much as possible in their natural state.

"Giving money is wonderful," the president said, "but giving your heart to an effort sometimes works miracles." He expressed the hope that children in particular would learn from Sarah's story that individuals can make a difference but that there are often failures and disappointments along the way and it is important not to give up.

The Eco Hero award consists of a $50,000 donation to an environmental project of the recipient's choice, and a gold medal inscribed with the constellation Ursa Minor, or Little Bear. The North Star, to which the constellation points, appears on the medal in the form of a diamond chip.

When the Eco Hero medal was presented to her, Sarah Stewart said her effort was successful because so many people cared and helped. She wanted to thank them all. Especially her mother.